Billion Dollar Favor

Alix Vaughn

Copyright © 2023 by Alix Vaughn

All rights reserved.

No portion of this book may be reproduced in any form without written permission from the publisher or author, except as permitted by U.S. copyright law.

Contents

1. Chapter 1 — 1
2. Chapter 2 — 8
3. Chapter 3 — 20
4. Chapter 4 — 27
5. Chapter 5 — 33
6. Chapter 6 — 43
7. Chapter 7 — 55
8. Chapter 8 — 68
9. Chapter 9 — 79
10. Chapter 10 — 82
11. Chapter 11 — 94
12. Chapter 12 — 101
13. Chapter 13 — 107
14. Chapter 14 — 115
15. Chapter 15 — 125
16. Chapter 16 — 131
17. Chapter 17 — 134

18. Chapter 18 — 142
19. Chapter 19 — 147
20. Chapter 20 — 156
21. Chapter 21 — 160
22. Chapter 22 — 165

About Author — 169

Chapter 1

Max

I've always run Journey Studios as a laid-back company. But on this Tuesday afternoon it was a bit *too* laid-back for my liking. It was early afternoon, at that. And with less than a month until the new game dropped, I needed everyone to focus. But that would only work if *I* could focus, and I was currently meandering down a rabbit hole of memories.

One memory in particular, the night Kate, Steven, Lacey and I went skinny dipping at Bolton Pond. I say 'skinny dipping' but really, Steven and I had just stripped down to our boxers and Lacey and Kate shucked off their jeans.

That night the moon had been full and the weather was gorgeous. It was our senior year and I hadn't seen Lacey for a week and a half. Her boyfriend, Craig, was off visiting a college he was interested in. Some fancy college on the east coast that I didn't care to know the name of.

As we swam in the pond, the warm water lapping at our skin, my mind was full of worries. If Craig was heading east, would Lacey follow him?

She was my best friend, but we rarely saw one another these days thanks to all of her time being monopolized by Craig. We hadn't talked about what would happen once summer was over, not since our early years of daydreaming about what the future might hold.

Me, well…I wasn't going to college. Most days I fought back the anxiety of having absolutely no idea what I was doing.

"Hey," Steven said, gliding through the water and passing me, "I'm going to grab towels out of my car. Gotta have Kate home soon."

I nodded, watching as Kate and Lacey played around, laughing, a little further out in the pond. The moonlight left silver ripples on the dark surface of the water. I wanted to sear this moment in my mind forever, but didn't want to keep the bittersweet undertone of it.

Not long after, Kate splashed me with a grin. "She's all yours, Maxie."

I hated when she called me that, but any kind of retort stuck in my throat as I turned and saw Lacey swimming toward me. Her hair was soaked from the chin down, plastered to her jaw and throat. Despite the warm air, when she was close enough I saw her shiver.

"You okay?" I asked. "I have an extra sweatshirt in my car."

She nodded, mouth dipping under the water momentarily. "Yeah, that would be nice. I think I've just been in too long. I'm starting to get pruney."

I opened my mouth to respond, but Kate called out, letting us know that they were leaving.

"We should probably get going, too," I sighed. I kicked off the murky bottom of the pond and did a lazy backstroke, keeping an eye on Lacey. She followed with a shy smile, water lapping at her shoulders and collarbones.

When we reached the shallow water I clambered out and looked back to ask if she needed a towel.

But the words never made it out of my mouth.

She stepped out of the water like a goddess, rivulets pouring down her skin and clinging to her curves. She pushed her hair out of her face and I couldn't stop staring. Thank God she was momentarily distracted with finding a spot to sit and put her jeans back on. The white shirt she wore did little to hide her body now that it was soaked. The swell of her breasts was accentuated, *and I got a quick glimpse of her black lace-trimmed underwear. I felt myself harden and quickly wrapped a towel around my waist to hide the evidence.*

Did she wear those for Craig? Had he touched her, taken them off her...?

My mind went blank and blood rushed in my ears. Would this be the night I would finally make a move? As if in slow-motion, her eyes lifted to meet mine.

The intercom on my desk buzzed and I jerked, accidentally kicking over the trash can.

Tara, my assistant, spoke nervously through the connection: "Victor is asking if you're going to make it, or if he should start without you."

I let out a guttural sigh, dropping my head and hitting the button to open the speaker system. "Tell him I'll be there in a few. Just gathering my notes."

With that, I stood from my desk and shook off memories of the past.

"Hey," I called, popping my head into the staff breakroom and interrupting what looked like an intense game of foosball. "Big meeting in a few minutes - can you guys turn the tunes down?"

Stacy and Dev, two of my audio engineers, along with Oliver, a game auditor, all apologized. Dev leaned over and poked the Bluetooth speaker until it dropped in volume.

"Long lunch?" I asked breezily, not wanting to be a hard ass, but needing them to understand that we all had to be on our toes. The trio shared guilty looks. I liked to give my employees some freedom. It helped with creativity and the overall morale. However, sometimes the whip needed to be cracked.

"We're heading back in a few," Stacy explained. "Sorry, Max."

"No problem. Just make sure you have all the licenses for the first half of the game's audio sorted out by the end of the week, yeah?"

I left them to it, rushing because now I was going to be late to my own meeting.

It was crunch time. Journey hadn't released a new, big-name game in the past year and a half, so *Apocalypse Summit* had to go off without a hitch.

Unfortunately, people like Stacy, Dev and Oliver got to do all the fun stuff. Me, on the other hand…

I stepped into the conference room with an apologetic smile. Victor looked a little too smug about my late arrival and was already standing at his spot to the right of my seat, at the head of the table.

"Sorry, Max. Got started without you since we're on a tight schedule," he explained with a grin. Victor was a year or two younger than me, and full of himself. There was no reason he couldn't have waited a few minutes for me to arrive. He just wanted to highlight the fact that I was late.

"No problem," I replied, giving my financial crew a nod and a smile. "Carry on, I'll catch up."

As Victor jumped back into where we were as far as budgeting, and what marketing projections looked like, I couldn't help zoning out. After all, I'd been doing this for over a decade. My first major game, *Fatal Moon*, had been a crash course in what not to do when breaking into the video game industry. But it had still been popular enough to earn a few awards and bring in steady money. No complaints there.

Back then I was nineteen and full of high hopes and big goals. And I'd accomplished most of them. These days, in my thirties, all I wanted was to make Journey Studios lucrative and relevant enough to support the employees. And maybe every few years, throw something fresh into the mix—something that challenged the norm.

The tough part was balancing that creativity with the boring, logistical aspects of owning a company. Like meeting with the financial team.

Only fifteen minutes in, my phone buzzed. I dug it out of my jacket pocket and glanced at the screen. **Gilead Elementary**.

Why would Rosie's school be calling me right now? Never a good thing. I groaned internally and excused myself.

Victor nodded solemnly, but I could see the glee in his eyes. Sometimes I wondered if I'd made a mistake hiring him five years ago. But he was one of the best designers in the industry, that was undeniable. Even if he was looking for a way to usurp my throne every single day, he was a valuable asset.

"Hello?"

"Mr. Munroe. I'm sorry to interrupt you at work, but since Ann is no longer listed as an emergency contact—"

"Yes," I muttered, pacing down the hallway and giving tight smiles to those I passed. "Yes, Ann is no longer Rosie's nanny, and I haven't found a replacement yet—"

"Right, well, again, I'm sorry to bother you, but Rosie appears to be running a fever and we can't let her return to class."

Ducking into my office, I closed the door and let my head drop. Another day of work interrupted, though it couldn't be helped.

"Okay. It'll take me about twenty minutes to get there, is that alright?"

"Of course, Mr. Munroe. No rush. We'll keep her comfortable until you arrive."

I thanked the secretary and hung up with a sigh. It wasn't Rosie's fault, or even her ex-nanny's, that we were in this situation. Ann had gotten into a nasty accident crossing the street on her day off over a month ago. She'd needed extensive surgery, bad enough that it was clear she wouldn't be returning to work anytime soon.

But what I'd told the school had been a partial lie; I did, in fact, have a replacement for Ann. She just hadn't started yet.

My heartbeat picked up at the thought. I shook my head, trying to ignore the residual adrenaline rush of my youth—and the memory I'd been happily wallowing in less than an hour ago.

So what if Lacey Weaver, my childhood best friend, had agreed to help out for a few months until I found someone permanent?

It was just Lace. We'd known each other since we were in first grade. *Just Lace.*

But the thought conjured her features, and I took a deep, slow breath remembering. The crinkles at the side of her huge blue eyes when she smiled, her dimples, the way she laughed at the most unexpected things.

We hadn't seen each other in person since high school graduation. Lacey had run off to college and I'd...well, I'd started Journey Studios. Set the headquarters in Cold Springs, a city that was hard to imagine Lacey in. She was definitely a small-town girl. It hadn't surprised me at all when, after reconnecting, she'd told me she was a librarian.

As a kid Lace had been quiet, shy, and very smart.

But that was a decade ago; we were adults now. I had a kid. And if this was going to work—I *needed* it to work—I had to rid myself of those echoing *what ifs*.

What is was what mattered. Rosie mattered.

"Hey," I said, stepping briefly back into the conference room, "I'm sorry—I need to go pick my daughter up from school. I probably won't be returning for the rest of the day," a quick glance at Victor revealed just how thrilled he was at that, "but, Steven, can you update me later?"

Steven, as well as his wife Kate, were also old friends of mine and Lacey's. We'd all gone to school together, but I'd pulled Steven into the business early on. He was my chief financial officer, and I knew I could rely on him to curb any crazy ideas that Victor decided to pitch while I went to get Rosie.

A quick dash back to my office to grab my laptop and bag and I was trotting toward the elevator. Steven popped up and grabbed me by the elbow.

"What's up? Everything okay?"

"Yeah," I sighed, glancing to make sure the call button was lit up, "Rosie's sick, her school called. I'll have to be home with her today, and maybe tomorrow if the fever doesn't clear up."

He grimaced. He had two kids of his own, much younger than Rosie. "Sorry, man. No replacement for Ann yet, then? You know Tara could probably field interviews if you were desperate."

"No, no, I couldn't do that to her. Besides…I might have someone who can step in. At least temporarily."

"Oh." Steven gave me an appraising look and I knew I was probably slowly turning red, from the neck up. Unfortunately I hadn't grown out of some habits. "Who did you find?"

"I'll tell you about her later," I dodged his question, dashing into the elevator and giving him a grin as the doors began to shut. He nodded and turned to go back to the meeting.

When he found out that Lacey Weaver was coming to Cold Springs to be a nanny for Rosie, he'd never let me live it down.

Which was why I had to keep it to myself for as long as I could.

At the very least, until she arrived a week from today.

Chapter 2

Lacey

Cold Springs wasn't quite what I expected. I should have done more research on the city but I had procrastinated, finding a million other things to occupy my time. Instead, I decided to just show up and wing it.

The airport was massive and people were bumping into each other, trying to get to their next destination. I filed out into the main area with all the other passengers, my eyes scanning my surroundings. Magazine and snack stores, a little book nook, overpriced vending machines. Nothing new.

And then I saw the sign with my name printed across it.

Lacey Weaver for Max Munroe.

My heart pounded at the insinuation, but I shook it off and tried to walk confidently toward the person holding it. Who was definitely *not* Max. Unless he'd shrunk quite a few inches in the last decade and lost most of his hair.

Smiling hesitantly, I made eye contact with the small older man.

"Hello, I'm Lacey—I think you're here for me?"

"Yes, Ms. Weaver. Let me take that." He shuffled forward, grasping the handle on my luggage. "My name is Gerald. I'm Mr. Munroe's driver."

Max had a driver? That shouldn't surprise me but it did.

"Unfortunately he was held up at work," Gerald continued to explain as he led me toward the exit of the airport. "However, he should arrive at the condo shortly after we do." He turned once we were outside, a smile lighting up his face. "Is this your first time in Cold Springs?"

"Um, yes. It is." I gazed out at the skyline, all buildings reflecting light. The airport was closer to downtown than I expected.

"Welcome, welcome. It's a beautiful city. I've lived here my whole life."

Gerald continued to chat as he carefully loaded my luggage, and me, into a Land Rover. Tucking myself into the backseat, I recalled Max's dream car when we were kids: a Pontiac Firebird. He'd lusted after a neighbor's, cherry red and rusted with an actual firebird detailed on the hood.

Now that he'd "made it," had he given up on those dreams? The Land Rover was tasteful and balanced, just not what I expected from him. But I really didn't know Max anymore. I looked forward to getting all caught up on what his life was like these days.

Gerald offered me bottled water, which I politely refused. He pulled out of the airport and wove seamlessly through the streets of Cold Springs, pointing out landmarks and areas of interest.

"The National Geology Museum is right there, in the dark brick building. This is the intellectual district, I'd say. Ah, see, just up the street? That's Mabel Humphrey Library. She was an advocate for literacy, an elementary teacher I believe, and the library was built in her honor about twenty years ago."

I barely glanced up, feeling my cheeks heat with embarrassment. Humphrey Library actually had a reputation as one of the best in the Midwest, so I should be thrilled to set eyes on it. But after losing my job at the much smaller Pratt Library, the last thing I wanted was to be reminded of how my life had taken a nosedive.

"Is it much further?" I asked, trying to turn the conversation. Gerald glanced at me in the rearview mirror.

"We're almost there, Mrs. Weaver—"

"Oh, call me Lacey, please. And it's just Miss, anyway."

Gerald's graying brows rose in interest, but thankfully, he had enough tact not to ask why a woman my age was unmarried. Not that it was totally uncommon these days, but most of the people we'd gone to high school with were married and had at least a few kids by now.

Even Max had jumped on that train. After all, his daughter was the whole reason I was here.

Anxiety made my heart rate pick up again and I gazed out the window, willing myself to calm down. *It's just Max—your old friend. There's nothing to be anxious about.*

But with Max, it had never been that simple. Even when we were growing up, I could remember moments of nervousness around him. Like that perfect summer day in junior year when we'd skipped class and gone to the town pool, instead. Caught up in laughter and the rush of summer coming soon, he had lifted me in his arms and I'd pressed myself against him to stay balanced. The memory of our wet, bare skin, crushed together, his curled lips, the sun warming us. Years later it was enough to send a shiver up my spine.

The trip down memory lane was interrupted by Gerald pulling up to a curb.

"Here we are," he announced, putting the Rover in park. "Skyside."

I slipped out of the SUV and thanked him as he handed me my luggage. "I'm sure I'll be seeing you soon, Miss. Oops, I mean, Lacey. Welcome, again, to Cold Springs. I hope you'll like it here."

"Thank you, Gerald. I appreciate it."

With a nod, Gerald heaved himself into the driver's seat and pulled carefully out into traffic. I clutched my new roller luggage, a surprisingly heavy duffle bag hanging off my shoulder, and stared up at Max's building.

Skyside was thirty-eight floors high. I knew that because he'd texted me a few days ago that he owned the penthouse on the top floor.

You'll have to take a special elevator, he'd warned. **But the staff can key in the code for you and then we'll get you a temporary card.**

Temporary. It was a stark reminder that my whole life felt temporary right now.

Maybe this would be a good change of pace. Maybe I needed a break from my career, anyway. I'd been at Pratt Library for seven years and was comfortable there, but the new director had really shaken things up. Not in a good way...

Maybe I'd dodged a bullet.

Taking a deep breath, I walked toward the building and smiled at the doorman who gave me a slight bow as I entered. The front desk was gorgeous, minimalist, and staffed with only two women. Both looked up at me with sharp, cold eyes that made my breath catch in my throat.

"Hello," I said after a moment, realizing that they weren't going to bother greeting me. The woman nearest me looked up and scanned me over, her mouth a perfectly straight line.

"Can I help you."

It was a statement, not a question; said in a dead tone that made me shrink internally.

"Um, yes. I'm here to see Max Munroe and he told me—"

This woman actually had the gall to roll her eyes. Just slightly, but I caught it. Annoyed, my own eyes narrowed. She picked up a clipboard and barely gave it a glance.

"I don't have any instructions here from Mr. Munroe stating that he was expecting a guest."

"Well, yes, that's because he was supposed to pick me up from the airport but—"

Before I could explain further, she interrupted, hair swinging severely along her jawline as she finally faced me. "We don't let just anyone in here."

My mouth snapped shut. A rush of hot anger filled my chest as I clutched the luggage handle tightly. But someone interrupted.

"She's not just anyone, Brianna. I didn't leave instructions because I was planning to bring her here myself."

Brianna's eyes widened and I half-turned, my heart stopping as I finally set eyes on Max.

He was as boyishly handsome as ever with that lopsided smile. In that moment, it felt like we were entirely alone—the rest of the room phased out and it was just the two of us. His smile was apologetic as he stood, hands in his pockets and hair in his eyes like always.

"Sorry, Lace," he said, stepping forward and reaching out to wrap a hand around the luggage handle—and my hand. I quickly slipped mine away, feeling my face heat.

Max's gaze dulled for a moment before the woman at the desk coughed. "Mr. Munroe, I'm sorry. It's our policy—"

"I'm aware," he said, not bothering to turn his attention to her. There was a cold edge to his voice that I'd never heard before. It hit me that I was seeing *the* Max Munroe, not my childhood friend, but the owner of a video game empire. A man who demanded respect.

Brianna's eyes dropped.

"I'm going to need an elevator card for her," he continued, turning his gaze away from me. I finally took a breath, clutching the duffle bag with both hands. "And she'll be here for a month, at least." His eyes darted to mine in question; we hadn't actually determined how long I'd be staying, although I was willing to stay as long as he wanted me—*needed* me.

As long as he needed me to watch his daughter, until he found a replacement.

Max led me toward a private hallway with just one recessed elevator. He held his wallet up to a little keypad and the light turned green. Somewhere in the distance, I heard the quiet hush of machinery heading our way.

"Sorry," he murmured, giving me another apologetic smile. "I didn't think to ask Gerald to walk you in, but I didn't think they'd be so rude, either."

"It's fine," I insisted. "Can't blame them." I looked down at what I was wearing, jeans that were a little ratty at the hem and a floral cotton blouse. My hair was probably a mess, too.

"You look great," Max said easily. But his eyes darted away from mine again, and I wondered if he meant it, or was just being polite.

The elevator arrived and we both stepped in. It was spacious, had an almost industrial feel to it—like you could move a grand piano if you had to. There was only one button, and he pushed it.

"Your flight was okay?"

I nodded, eyes on the metallic paneling. It was strange making small talk with someone who had been such a big part of my life. We were so close growing up, but this felt almost like talking to a stranger. Hopefully we'd get past that. I longed for the easygoing conversations, the laughter.

I sighed and he noticed, but didn't ask. The weight of the last few weeks was settling in now that the adrenaline rush was wearing off.

"Thank you again for this," Max offered. The elevator doors opened and we stood before a door. He opened it with a key and I followed him into a foyer. We were immediately in his apartment. Or, penthouse, rather, since it was literally bigger than most houses I knew. The foyer alone was massive, with gorgeous paintings on the walls and an elaborate light fixture above. He tucked my luggage to the side and took my duffle bag.

"Let me show you around first."

I followed him down a long hallway flanked by doorways that I couldn't get a good look into.

"This is the living area," he explained, doing a slow spin to face me and gesture to the open space.

All at once, my old crush came back like a punch in the gut. I could only nod, eyes glued to him as he pointed out a few essentials. The TV, huge sectional couches, a workspace if I needed it.

I had no intention of telling him that I was *out of* work. Not yet, anyway. Embarrassment seeped in with that breathless, heady feeling. It didn't feel great to be walking around Max's luxury penthouse while I was completely jobless except for my new temporary nanny job. Who got *fired* as a librarian?

"It's beautiful," I choked out, trying to sound breathlessly impressed instead of crushed by the weight of my long-hidden, unrequited love.

Not love, I corrected myself. *You were kids; it's been years. It was never love.*

He gave me that lopsided smile and turned, leading me into a surprisingly intimate dining room that looked out onto a nearby park (thirty-eight stories down) and a high-end kitchen. It wasn't overdone, which I appreciated. Realizing that Max was still Max and hadn't totally sold out to his wealthy image was a relief.

There were four bathrooms, one of which was attached to the master bedroom. We were both blushing as Max gave me a quick glimpse of his space. The bed was undone, which was maybe why he was embarrassed, but I found it endearing.

"Housekeeper couldn't make it in today?" I teased, shooting him a grin as he continued down the hallway. He winced.

"Actually, no. She only comes twice a week."

I couldn't help laughing as we stood outside of another bedroom. "Honestly, that's great," I reassured him. "There have definitely been days where I wished I had help. You've earned it."

He shrugged and I took a look into the room. It was a tastefully done bedroom, with a king sized bed and a long picture window. There was a mahogany dresser, a nightstand and a plush rug at the foot of the bed.

Then I saw the shelves of action figures.

"Oh, my gosh," I breathed, laughter bubbling up again. "I can't believe you still have these!"

Still in the doorway, Max rubbed the back of his neck. Lining a set of twelve shelves were boxed action figures, all from different franchises. I grinned at a Boba Fett, remembering long nights spent watching the entire Star Wars series. I'd inevitably fall asleep on his couch while he stayed up eating snacks, glued to the screen.

"Had to keep them for nostalgia's sake," he rumbled in a low voice. My gaze snapped back to him, a shiver running up my spine. "I really should find another place to store them."

It wasn't Max the kid I'd grown up with leaning in the doorway, but Max Munroe—industry mogul. The man who'd been on magazine covers, who cleaned up well in tailored suits but still had that mischievous smile.

That debilitating rush of anxiety and excitement took over my body. I bit my lip, trying to look away—he was long and lean, hands tucked into his pockets again. The light streaming in through the window lit up his eyes. They looked brown, but turned a gorgeous caramel color in the right conditions. It was almost too much to take.

"This is kind of weird, isn't it?" he asked quietly, a sad smile on his face.

My heart sank a little bit. Was he regretting asking me to come?

"I mean, that we're both so grown up now," he rushed out, straightening up. "Weird to see each other as adults. I never really thought about it as kids, but here we are."

"You're right," I admitted, taking a step toward him. "It is a little weird. Maybe because we haven't seen each other in person for so long—"

"I'm sorry about that," he interrupted, brows knit. "Really. I should have reached out more, kept in touch."

I shook my head. "No, that's on both of us. We let the time get away from us."

I didn't mention the other extenuating circumstances that had us slowly drifting apart. My relationship with my ex, who had never liked him. Max's budding fame, and then the whirlwind romance with Skylar West. Plus the few thousand miles between us…

"It doesn't matter," I insisted. "We're here now. We have time to catch up."

That sad smile was back again. But he only nodded in agreement. He opened his mouth to speak, but a clatter and shout stopped him.

Sticking his head out into the hallway, he called, "Rosie?"

"Dad!"

The sound of feet running down the hall had me on edge, breath caught.

This was the moment I'd meet Max's daughter. It felt bittersweet, facing the future he'd made for himself while we'd been apart. But then Rosie Munroe appeared in the doorway.

As soon as she saw me she quieted and tucked herself into his side, chewing nervously at her bottom lip. When she glanced up at him, I saw that they shared those same caramel-colored eyes.

"Rosie, this is my friend, Lacey," he introduced. "She's going to stay with us until we can find a replacement for Ann. So she'll be picking you up from school, taking you places—okay?"

Rosie nodded, then tugged on Max's t-shirt. He bent in half and I couldn't hide my grin at seeing him interact with his daughter. She whispered something in his ear.

"Yup," he answered. I watched the pair in confusion, feeling a little nervous about how Rosie would take to me.

"But this was your game room," Rosie said, sounding surprised.

He smiled in embarrassment, tugging her into a side-hug. "I know, hun, but Lacey's going to stay with us for a while so she needs her own room, right? Besides, I play games all day. I don't need a whole room for it here. I'll just spend more time with you."

That seemed to appease the little girl, though she looked skeptical as she shot me a glance. I smiled encouragingly at her. I'd started out my career at the library as a children's librarian, so I wasn't totally inept with kids. But I could tell that Rosie wasn't too sure about me and I didn't want to force it.

"Do you want to show Lacey the rest of the house?" Max asked, raising his eyebrows as he looked down at his daughter.

She mumbled a reply and grabbed his hand, but glanced back at me as we headed further down the hall. She pointed out the bathroom between our rooms and then reached the door all the way at the end of the hallway.

"This is my room," she said, her voice rising in confidence as Max pushed the door open softly. Rosie bounded in and jumped onto the bed. It was a classic girl's room, all pinks and pastels. There was a beautiful painting of a carousel horse hanging on one wall and a messy desk with lots of books and school supplies.

Rosie was looking at the two of us through her long lashes as I took in the room.

"This is a beautiful bedroom," I said, giving her a small smile. She picked up a stuffed animal and pressed it to her face, shy once more. That, we had in common, I'd been a pretty shy kid and still was, I suppose, as an adult.

"She's got her own alarm clock," he took over, nodding toward the little white nightstand, "so you won't have to worry about getting her up in the morning. And she's pretty good about picking out her own clothes, too. She might ask for help if she can't reach something in the closet."

Speaking of, that closet was the size of three closets. One of the doors was open and I could see two stacked rows of clothes hanging up. It was a little surprising that Max was so indulgent with so many clothes, but then, Rosie's mom was a model. Maybe she was around more than I'd been led to believe...

In the last few months of catching up through phone calls and texts, he had casually mentioned that while he and Skylar co-parented, he had full custody. Skylar had agreed to the arrangement readily. She traveled a lot for work and couldn't provide a stable home for Rosie, so Max had taken up the responsibility without a second thought.

It worked for them. Apparently Skylar visited when she could, but he had been vague about how often that actually happened.

A buzzing sound drew all of our attention and Max stiffened, digging his phone out of his pocket. His features dropped as soon as he got a glimpse of the screen. With a sigh, he excused himself and stepped out into the hallway.

"Hey. Yeah, I know they're asking for the final cuts of those scenes—I checked in with Dominic, he's responsible for them." There was a pause, and when he spoke next it was clear that he was annoyed and angry. "No,

I'm absolutely *not* coming in for that. I've barely been home an hour. I understand, but you're going to have to figure that out on your own—"

His voice slowly receded as Rosie and I were left alone in her room. She still held the stuffed animal, now loosely in her lap.

For a kid so young, there was an air of melancholy about her as she watched him walk away. I bit my lip. I'd known coming out here that things wouldn't be the same as they were a decade ago. As Max pointed out, we were both adults, with entire lives and responsibilities and years and years separating us...

What had I gotten myself into?

Chapter 3

Max

"All I'm saying is, I'm surprised you dated a model for so long and this is what you chose to dress your daughter in." Lacey laughs on the other end of the phone.

I leaned back in my office chair, chuckling to myself and imagining Lacey's face. She'd only been back in my life for three days, and already I felt more alive.

Was that a good thing or a sad revelation about my mental state? What did it mean that I only now felt like I was "waking up" to life?

"Her mother has nothing to do with it, and neither do I! Rosie has her own sense of style." I insisted, toying with the mouse to wake the computer screen up. I really should be looking over the financial sheets that the team had sent for signatures that morning. Instead, Lacey had called almost an hour ago to ask what Rosie liked for dinner and we'd lost track of time chatting.

Movement caught my attention near the door of my office, and I jumped.

"Uh, Lace, I'm sorry—I have to go, someone just stepped in."

I could hear the disappointment in her voice, which was oddly reassuring. Looked like I wasn't the only one who enjoyed our conversations then; it was a two-way street.

"Oh, okay. No problem, the grocery is only a few blocks away, right? Will you be back to eat with us or do you want me to keep a plate warm for you?"

Steven stepped into the office and I shot him a panicked look. He had an amused look on his face, meaning he knew who I was talking to.

"I'm not sure yet, but I'll text you and let you know. And don't feel like you have to get fancy. We've both been living off frozen chicken nuggets for a few weeks so, we'll be fine."

Lacey's chuckle warmed my heart, and I had to work hard to suppress the smile threatening to break through. We hung up and I turned my chair to fully face Steven, who stood leaning on the desk with that damn grin.

"So…you and Lacey are still keeping in touch, I see. I wasn't sure if you two would still gel like you used to."

My face heated. I hadn't told him yet—or his wife, Kate—that Lacey was here, in Cold Springs. Guilt made me fidget with a few papers on the desk until I could meet his eyes. But a part of me had also wanted to keep her to myself for a little bit…to bask in the memory of how easy being friends with her was.

"Actually…"

Steven's eyes narrowed, the grin gone. "Uh oh. Something wrong with the financial reports? I can take a look—"

He sat down, leaning forward. I sighed and ran a hand through my hair; it was almost time for a haircut. I'd caught Lacey glancing at my messy locks more than once over the last few days.

"No, no, nothing like that. Everything looks good so far. I think we'll be set for the release unless any unexpected snags come up." I cleared my throat, sitting up and doing my best to put on a dominant attitude; the one I'd learned to fake years ago. Raising my eyes to meet his, I said, "It's about Lacey. She's here, in town. And she's staying with me."

Steven's eyes widened and he sat back in surprise. There was a long moment as he processed the information.

"I...what? Lacey's here? And she's with you? Like, *with* you with you or—"

I shook my head vigorously, praying that I wouldn't turn bright red at even the mention of me and Lacey being more than friends. There was a rushing sound in my ears, reminiscent of those nervous moments I'd had around her in high school when my unexpected crush suddenly popped up. It didn't help that he and his wife had a theory that Lacey and I were soulmates, and both in serious denial.

But she had never shown an interest in me back then. She was just doing me a favor, helping out an old friend—that's all we were. *Friends.*

"No. Definitely not like that. She's here for Rosie."

Now Steven's brows creased in confusion. "Rosie? Why?" Then the lightbulb clicked. "Wait, the new nanny is *Lacey*?"

I winced, knowing it sounded bad. Even before reaching out to her, I'd spent more than a few nights pacing back and forth, worrying that she'd take it the wrong way. But if I asked as a favor...of course I'd compensate her for her time, knowing it would take her away from her job for a while. But she'd been quick to reassure me that her job wasn't a problem and she was more than happy to help.

Still, I didn't want her feeling like *the nanny*. She was more than that.

With a sigh, I admitted, "Yeah, kind of. It's not permanent. She's just helping out until I can find someone who will be a good fit. You know, it's been crazy the last few weeks with *Apocalypse* releasing soon and having to keep an eye on Rosie by myself."

He nodded, managing to look sympathetic. But curiosity lingered in his eyes as he watched me closely.

"So how long is she here for, then?"

I shrugged. "I'm not sure. She just got here a few days ago, and I was planning on talking to her about the best way to set up interviews when I get a free moment. Which, you know…"

"You don't *have* a free moment."

"Exactly. That's why she's helping out. Hopefully we can get it all figured out quickly."

I tipped my chin up, trying to appear assured and in control. That worked with most people at Journey, but the problem was, Steven *knew* me. Really knew me.

He'd been there for some pretty tough times in my life growing up, my dad passing away after years of drinking too much, my struggle with the decision not to go to college, and yeah…that suffocating crush I'd had on Lacey for a year or two.

Like it's gone now? a small voice in my head asked. Now wasn't the time to be thinking about this.

So what if hearing her laugh at my jokes made me smile? So what if catching her falling asleep last night while watching a movie with Rosie and me had made my heart ache?

*She's only here to help out a **friend**,* I reminded myself.

As if he'd heard the internal conversation, Steven frowned.

"It's not a big deal," I insisted before he could open his mouth.

"Sure it's not, Max. She only flew to Cold Springs to help you out." He tried to hide a chuckle. "How's she doing, by the way? Seems weird that she can drop everything on a dime like that."

"She seems fine. I was worried about that, too, but she keeps telling me it's not a big deal. Maybe she had a lot of PTO saved up?" I said awkwardly. As the owner of a big company, I really didn't know much about what it was like to hold a "normal" job.

Steven sat back, fingers grazing his chin as he thought. "I wonder how she and Craig ended up," he mused.

I clenched my teeth in annoyance. Lacey's high school boyfriend, Craig, hadn't been a good guy. At least I hadn't thought so at the time. He was very controlling. That was a nice way of putting it.

For most of our senior year, we'd watched her scramble at his beck and call. Although she never admitted it, it always seemed like she could never do enough to make him happy. He was always rolling his eyes in disappointment, ignoring her when his friends were around, or outright leaving her at school a few times when he was supposed to be her ride. Luckily, I'd been driving my dad's old Toyota at the time and had lingered around after school long enough to be able to offer her a ride without making a big deal of it.

All these years later, my chest tightened at the memory of her slumped shoulders and that air of defeat. But she hadn't broken up with him. We graduated and they were still together.

"I don't know what happened with them," I admitted. "I didn't ask when we got back in touch."

He snorted. "Well, I'm assuming that if they were still together or even talking, you'd know. That creep would never let her get anywhere near you, do you remember?"

I frowned. *How could I forget?* Steven continued to ramble, crossing his arms.

"—Kate telling me that Craig told Lacey he didn't like her hanging out with us. That's why she wasn't around so much senior year."

I blinked in surprise. "Wait, really? I thought that was just his personality."

He sighed, shaking his head. "It's crazy how blind you always were. Craig definitely had it out for you. I don't know if he ever said it straight out, but he didn't want her around you at all." A slow smirk crept up his face. "Maybe he could sense what *we* all could."

I rolled my eyes and pushed back from the desk, standing.

"Alright, alright. Let's not dig up the past; you're right, they're probably not still together, and it's her business anyway."

"You're not going to ask her?"

"Why would I?" I huffed. "I'm sure she'll bring it up at some point."

He stood too, watching me closely once more. "If she's in Cold Springs and staying with you, I'm willing to bet she's single. No man in his right mind would be okay with his woman staying with a millionaire."

Billionaire, I almost corrected, but humility kept me in check. Besides, as head of my financial team, he knew exactly how much I made.

"Listen, I have to go check on the team," I sighed, herding him toward the door.

He shot me a sly glance over his shoulder. "Well the good news is, now that you two are in close quarters you can finally find out how she really feels about you."

My face twisted in annoyance. "I'm telling you, *there's nothing there*."

On her end, at least. Was I still harboring a bit of a crush…? Maybe.

"Sure," he drawled. "It all comes out in the end." He said the words heavily, hands raised, as if he were summoning something or speaking prophecy. I raised my eyebrows and chuckled.

"Aisha is going to kill me if I don't get to her office on time."

"And *Kate* is going to kill me if I don't get Lacey's number from you," he warned. "Don't think I've forgotten that you kept this little secret from me."

"She's only been here for three days!"

He shook his head. "Which only convinces me that there is something going on, Max. Or else you would've mentioned it the second you knew she was coming to the city. But, hey, deny it all you want."

We stepped into the hallway and parted ways, the guilt I'd been feeling for the last few days finally subsiding. Steven knew, and he'd let Kate know now, too. Would she be happy to hear from them? Absolutely!

She knew that I'd hired Steven soon after starting Journey Studios. I'd mentioned him a few times in passing, too, so it wasn't like Kate reaching out would be a surprise.

Now that the anxiety of getting this all off my chest was gone, it felt good to think about getting the gang back together. Maybe, if I could free up some time in my schedule, we'd all be able to go out for a drink and catch up properly. And maybe a glass of wine or two would lead to a conversation about how she and Craig had ended...

Because I was sure they were no longer together, which was a relief.

Not because I still had a thing for her, just because... well, because he hadn't been the right guy for her. Growing up with Lacey, I knew her better than most people. Did we still have some catching up to do as adults? Definitely.

But still. she was too good for Craig. In fact, if I really thought about it, I couldn't imagine Lace with anyone. She was just too *good*, too smart and funny and generous.

And I was lucky to have her here. Which was why I planned on totally ignoring the inkling of a crush that was starting up all over again.

Lacey Weaver was my friend and I'd spent too many years out of touch with her. I couldn't lose her now that she was back in my life.

I'd do anything I could to keep her right here.

Chapter 4

Lacey

Rosie kept giving me suspicious glances as she sat cross-legged by the living room coffee table. I was curled up on the couch, a book in hand. But I was doing the same; sneaking looks at her over the top of my glasses.

I'd been in Cold Springs for almost a week and Rosie still wasn't sure about me. I couldn't blame her. A strange woman showing up out of nowhere and living in your house—actually, she seemed pretty poised considering the situation. It could definitely be worse.

Besides, Max probably had all kinds of women snooping around, looking for a date, looking for a potential meal ticket in this city where nothing came cheap. I'd already gleaned through some apartment listings that the rent here was high enough to dissuade people like me from ever ordering out or doing any therapy shopping.

"How's your homework going?" I asked casually, keeping my eyes on my book. In my peripheral, she stopped writing for a moment as if sizing up the question.

"Okay," she said evasively.

Part of me wanted to offer help if she needed it, but I didn't want to offend her. Rosie seemed like a capable kid. Independent. Was that because he wasn't around much?

In the five days I'd been here, it was striking to me that I saw Rosie much more than Max did. It obviously bothered him, I'd caught a few of the sad looks he gave his daughter when they parted in the morning, Rosie scuffing her shoes on the ground as he lugged his work duffle over his shoulder. He practically lived at the office.

"It's all this craziness with the new release," he'd explained to me, an edge of anxiety in his voice. But Rosie had shot him a look that made me think that even if it *was* crazy at work right now, when it wasn't, he still didn't get to spend much more time at home.

Turning my attention back to my book, Rosie and I ignored each other for a few more minutes. Eventually she flipped her folder shut and stood with a little bounce.

"I'm done," she announced, walking over to the side table to pick up the TV remote.

Should I ask to look her homework over? Make sure she actually did it?

No, I didn't want to cross boundaries yet, not until she trusted me. Giving her a small smile, I half-paid attention to the book in my lap while keeping an ear out.

Rosie flipped through the TV channels restlessly, chewing on a chipped pink polished nail. The drop of the remote caught my attention. With a quick glance, I tried to read her emotions. She stared at the TV impassively, reacting neither positively nor negatively.

I kept my book open, but looked on the screen. Skylar West, Rosie's mom, was strutting down a catwalk. My eyes widened.

"Oh. That's...your mom, right?" I asked, mentally hitting myself for sounding so stupid. Rosie didn't take her eyes off the TV, but nodded. "Do you know where that is?" I asked, scanning the screen for any info. It was Live, I knew that much.

"No," Rosie chirped, eyes glued to her mom. I followed her gaze and couldn't look away either.

Skylar West was tall and leggy. Lean and small-chested, her skin was a beautiful, natural tan that Rosie's showed a hint of. Rosie had definitely inherited Skylar's wild, curly, dark hair, the same way she'd inherited her dad's eyes. But on screen, Skylar's hair was long and fell past her waist in thick, loose braids. Rosie's was chopped off at her shoulders and often sprung out of hair ties.

As we watched, Skylar reached the end of the catwalk, hit a pose, and turned back. Her hips sashayed seductively as she went. My face colored as I recalled the beginning of their relationship years ago.

When I went off to college with Craig in tow, Max and I didn't talk often. But I couldn't help keeping an eye on him. And even if I hadn't wanted to, it was impossible not to see him here and there. In the newspaper, giving interviews, in tabloids.

The latter was my first introduction to Skylar. **Stunning Model Captures Gaming Mogul's Heart**, the headline had read at the time. I'd scrunched my nose, finding it hard to think of Max as a "mogul." But by then Journey Studios and his first game, *Fatal Moon*, had taken off.

The photo on the front of the magazine was of Skylar and Max at an outdoor café. Skylar's long legs were stretched out, crossed at the ankles, as she and Max laughed. His hair had been tousled. Even up against Skylar West he was handsome, with that boyish grin and the dimple in his left cheek...

My heart had ached momentarily before I shut it down. At the time, I was still with Craig. It'd been harder than I thought to get rid of him. Two semesters in, Craig dropped out and spent most of his time hanging around the dorm despite having to get an apartment in town. I'd come back exhausted from class to him playing video games with my roommates' boyfriends, shouting and knocking things over in their excitement.

Where had it all gone wrong? Probably when I realized that Craig was perfectly fine riding my coat tails, which was a ridiculous idea. It's not like librarians made much and I knew if we got an apartment together, I'd be forking over most of the rent. He had zero work ethic and, as the years went by, was less and less attractive to me.

When we were out girls still looked his way and sent him flirty glances, but I ignored it, no longer jealous. They could have him if they wanted him. Part of me had been secretly waiting for him to cheat. It'd be an easy out. But he never did or, at least, I never caught him.

And then... then my dad had passed. Unexpectedly, abruptly. A heart attack despite his years as a runner. Two months after his last marathon it happened when he and my mom were out getting coffee. He'd hadn't suffered, at least. It had been so quick. In the confusion, mom requested an autopsy and we found out that his heart had been scarred by another recent, small heart attack. But he'd never mentioned any pain or worries to us, so how could we have known?

Losing my dad was just too much. I lost my patience with Craig, and within weeks after the funeral I cut him loose. We argued so much and he was so ungrateful, so annoyed by my grief. It was a bitter breakup. Right about that same time, Skylar and Max were welcoming their daughter—Rosie.

It was strange back then to think of Max having a child, especially when I was so far off the path I had hoped for in life. I was single, about to graduate college with a lackluster degree, no prospects in my future.

Meanwhile he was blazing a creative path through the video game industry and getting followed by paparazzi.

Even pregnant, Skylar had managed to look absolutely gorgeous. I spent a year being depressed, jealous, and feeling like I lost out... until I started going to therapy. Mom suggested it and at first, I refused, but then she said she'd been going since my dad passed. That was the straw that broke the camel's back, and I gave in. If mom was willing to do better, than I should be, too.

In fact, mom was doing amazing. She and my father were so in love that I thought losing him would absolutely devastate her. And it did.

But she didn't stop living. She retired, then spent a year traveling with a few girlfriends. She had hobbies, got together with a Thursday night book club, and occasionally mentioned a handsome man here or there. It still broke my heart a little bit that she was moving on, but I understood. I wished I could move on, too.

As I was healing, Max's life began to fall apart. At least that's how the media portrayed it. In reality, since I'd gotten to Cold Springs, he seemed to be doing well enough. His company had grown exponentially, and he had Rosie.

That was one thing he hadn't had to fight Skylar on, at least. When we finally caught up after years of being disconnected, I'd hesitantly asked about that situation. He'd revealed that Skylar had been willing to give Rosie up almost entirely right away, recognizing that the traveling life of a model wouldn't be suited for a toddler. And Skylar didn't want to give up her career.

It was hard to judge her for that, especially when she'd obviously made the right choice. Rosie deserved a stable home.

But a small voice in my mind reminded me that "stable" was relative. Was it really stable if he was never home? If Rosie spent most of her time with her nanny, and now, me? A woman she didn't trust.

Rosie flipped the channel again, this time to some animal documentary that looked a little gruesome. I blinked away the past, trying to focus on the present. And then I decided to jump in—if we were going to get to know each other, I, as the adult, needed to take the lead.

"Do you miss your mom?" I asked.

Rosie glanced at me and shrugged. "Sometimes."

I nodded, trying to be understanding. She didn't seem upset about it, but rather... numb? "Do you get to spend time with her sometimes?"

The next look from the eight-year-old was longer and I could tell that she was suspicious of my questions.

"Yeah. She goes to Capri every summer and I go with her. I like it there." She perked up a little, straightening and turning her attention from the TV to me. "Capri has cats *everywhere*. They walk along the walls and in the streets, and you can walk right up and pet them. They're so friendly."

I couldn't help smiling at her enthusiasm. "Really? That sounds cool. I never had a cat growing up, or any pets. My mom was allergic."

Rosie sighed, drooping back into the couch. "Me neither. Dad won't let me get a kitten. He says we're not home enough to take care of it."

I raised a brow as she pouted, bringing her knees up to her chin. Weren't home enough? Rosie was definitely home enough. Maybe this was something I could talk him into, and win Rosie over with, too. A win-win situation.

"Who knows what the future holds," I intoned, watching as Rosie cracked a small smile. She tucked herself back into the couch, leaning towards me a little bit.

It was a start.

I kept the book open in my lap and we both watched as a British narrator droned on about giant tortoises.

Chapter 5

Max

The whole elevator ride, I counted from one to ten, over and over. Years ago, Skylar had convinced me to try out yoga, but the only thing I got out of contorting my body into uncomfortable poses was learning to control my breathing and find moments of peace.

Today, that seemed impossible.

When I returned from meeting with Aisha, Journey Studio's head of marketing, my assistant Tara hesitantly flagged me down. Tara was straight out of college—actually, a drop out. She'd been going for graphic design, but couldn't let go of her *actual* dream. She'd been working for me for about a year and I could tell already that someday, with the right support, she'd be an intimidating rival in the industry. And I was happy to help her on her way.

After all, Journey couldn't be the end-all for video game design and development. Someday new blood would take over.

"What's up?" I'd asked, surprised because Tara was pretty quiet and handled things herself. I rarely had to chime in or make minor decisions. But the look on her face told me that something was very wrong.

"Can we talk?" she asked quietly, leaning toward me over her desk. "In your office, maybe?"

My office opened up onto a work floor. I liked being able to see and interact with the staff throughout the day, and Tara acted as a gatekeeper to my actual office. I scanned the floor, wondering if eyes were on us—what had her spooked? And then waved her in.

"Yeah, of course."

The door shut behind us, but Tara continued to fidget. My eyes narrowed as I took her in, trying to figure out where this was going.

"Is everything okay?" I asked slowly, rounding my desk to grab my bag. It was just after 6 p.m. and way past time I got home.

"Not really," Tara confessed, pulling her phone out of her back pocket. I watched as she tapped and scrolled before turning the screen to face me.

A gaming review site had an article about *Apocalypse Summit*. Not unusual, but the screengrab at the top of the article was.

Because it was right out of the *unreleased* game.

"How'd they get this?" I demanded, taking the phone and scanning through the article quickly.

"I don't know," Tara rushed out. "But it has to be someone in the office. It's one of the base designs, right? So…"

So it could be anyone.

This design had been submitted months ago and was just a base to build off of. A concept. The finished design looked really different, but I didn't feel good about this being out there.

"Someone leaked it."

Tara bit her lip. I handed her phone back and sighed, running a hand through my hair. I'd done it so much today that it felt oily, and with irritation, I realized I'd need a second shower today.

"There aren't any details," Tara pressed, "and I searched other sites—not just the popular ones, either. But there's a snitch in the office somewhere."

We both looked out through the glass wall at the twenty or so staff that worked on this floor. They were clueless, chatting or going about their business, earbuds in or eyes focused on their screens as they worked.

My jaw clenched. "Does anyone else know?"

Tara shook her head. I'd have to tell Steven about this. And Dominic. Better if I let them both know before I left…

So I had, and it was now past 7 p.m. Closing the penthouse door behind me, I took a deep breath. I was finally home. And something smelled delicious.

I walked into the kitchen, scanning the counter for food. My stomach was rumbling. I'd had to pass on lunch earlier in the day. Rosie's feet pattered against the tiled floor as she ran into the room and flung herself at me, arms wrapping around my waist.

"Hey baby girl," I murmured, trying not to clench my jaw. She was already in her pajamas and, from the sound of the TV on in the background, probably getting in one last show before bed.

"We made dinner," Rosie gushed, looking up at me. "Lacey roasted a—" she looked over her shoulder, at Lace, who had stepped into the room and was smiling softly at us. She was in PJs as well—a silk set that settled over her curves in a way that made me shiver. I peeled my eyes away from her and tried to focus on my daughter's chatter.

She dragged me toward the oven, bouncing on her feet as she explained that they'd roasted an entire chicken and Rosie had cut up the vegetables. "And there's ice cream for dessert!" she exclaimed, clearly riding a sugar high.

I looked up at Lacey from my place crouched on the ground. "That sounds amazing, hon." Scooping Rosie up, I let my bag drop to the floor. "But if you ate ice cream, did you brush your teeth? You don't want to get cavities."

Rosie argued for only a moment before sighing and going limp in my arms. I let her down with a chuckle and watched her scamper off toward the bathroom. She was leaning against the kitchen island, looking the exact opposite of how I felt.

Seeing her comfortable and relaxed in my home made me realize how rarely I got to feel the same way. Every day—including a lot of weekends—I came home stressed out and stiff. My neck had a kink that had persisted for months now, and I was barely sleeping.

The irritation and frustration from the day slowly seeped back in, darkening my demeanor as I picked up my bag and tossed it onto the bench near the door. Lacey watched silently, but her brow creased as I stomped around.

"I'm going to go ask Rosie if she wants to read before bed," she said slowly, standing on bare feet and padding toward the hallway.

I breathed deeply through my nose, knowing I was being an ass, but unable to stop my bad mood from snowballing. Over the next fifteen minutes I managed to get in a quick shower, change, and put my work bag away properly in my office space.

In the kitchen she sat at the island with a book of her own. Not surprising; she always had a book with her when we were growing up. The familiarity of it softened me a bit, but I banged around the kitchen, opening and closing the refrigerator door a few times and muttering to myself.

"There's a plate in the oven for you," she said tentatively, looking up at me through her glasses.

"Thanks," I bit out, opening the oven door and peeking inside. A waft of that wonderful smell surrounded me as I gingerly took the plate out, removing the foil. Roasted chicken and veggies, like Rosie had said.

"Did she already go to sleep?" I asked, sitting across from Lacey. My back and neck felt stiff and I rubbed at them, trying again not to clench my teeth.

Lacey watched me closely. "She did," she replied. "Well, sort of. I'm pretty sure she's reading under the covers, but there are worse problems to have." She gave me a small smile that I didn't return.

My mind was back at the office. Tomorrow Steven and I were meeting first thing, and unfortunately Victor would be there too.

"What's up?" she asked, putting aside her book.

I paused and glanced up at her. "Nothing," I said shortly. "It was a long day."

My annoyance hung over me like a dark cloud. The lights in the apartment were low and created an amber glow over the silk of her pajamas. There was nothing daring about the long-sleeved top she wore, but it still drew my eye, and I had to consciously look away and down at my plate.

She sighed. "I know you, Max. Something is bothering you."

"It's nothing," I insisted, waving her off, mouth full of chicken. "Just work."

"Okay... but, you know, work is a big part of your life. So if something's wrong—"

"Nothing's wrong," I snapped, surprising us both.

The silence after my outburst was deafening. Lacey stared at me with wide eyes and my heart plummeted at the hurt I saw there.

Her eyes narrowed and she straightened her shoulders, pushing her glasses up her nose. "Maxwell Munroe, if you don't apologize or tell me what's going on, you're going to go to bed feeling like trash and it'll ruin your whole day tomorrow."

She spoke in a sharp tone, the kind of tone I heard teachers at Rosie's school use to get kids in line. It had the same quelling effect on me, and I paused with my fork mid-way to my mouth. With a sigh, I put it down.

"You're right. I'm sorry. It was a really rough day."

"Do you want to talk about it?" she asked, and my mind was sent back to a decade ago—when we'd hang out after school and she'd ask the same thing, in the same tone of voice.

I hadn't known what I wanted to do after high school. My mom wanted me to go to college, was really pushing for it, but all I knew was that I *didn't* want to do that.

I'd been torn up about it all senior year. Especially because Lacey knew exactly what she wanted to do. And if I didn't go to college with her, we wouldn't see each other.

That part of my assumption turned out to be true. It was strange to set eyes on her so many years later, as adults. But I couldn't help appreciatively looking her over as she tucked a strand of hair behind her ear and waited for my answer.

"Alright," I gave in, wanting to focus on something other than how good she looked. *Fresh, as if she took a shower right before I got home. She probably smells amazing...*

Shaking the thought off, I filled her in on what Tara had found. Lacey caught on quickly, frowning as I pulled the article up on my phone and showed it to her.

"So," she said slowly, peering closely at the screenshot that had been taken from our designs, "someone leaked this, on purpose, ahead of the release. You have no idea who it could be?"

I shook my head. "Not really, no. We have over two hundred people working at Journey in all different areas. And this... this is a sketch, essentially, something that a lot of people have access to."

"So it isn't necessarily someone higher up?" Lacey's sharp eyes met mine as she went into full-on problem-solving mode. "What could they gain by leaking an old design that wasn't even finalized?"

I shrugged. "Money, probably. Game design is a competitive market, and Journey always comes up with something new that stands out. Our competitors don't like that. We're always one step ahead of them. By leaking preliminary designs, this person was probably paid well and, if there's any way to track them, our competitors will find them and offer them even more."

"But you're so close to the release," she insisted, sitting back. "And your company does so much for its employees. Who would want to betray you?"

"Someone who's unhappy with me," I sighed. "For whatever reason... or just greedy. I don't know."

I stared at my phone's screen, thinking of Victor... how he'd seemed both disappointed and excited by the news when I'd called him into Steven's office earlier that day.

"What's that look?" she asked, squinting at me.

I groaned and pressed my palms to my eyes, exhaustion finally settling in. "There's this guy... he's kind of my second-in-command. He's the lead designer..."

Lacey's head tilted to the side as she thought aloud, "You don't trust him. But if he's your lead designer, wouldn't he release something more updated? You said this is from months ago."

"Yeah, that's true. I don't know. Vic isn't always the brightest, but then, I think he'd be smart enough not to get caught. So he could've leaked something old on purpose."

We sat in silence for a few moments, both contemplating the options. The release was close, and I had a busy schedule ahead of me. A few interviews—Aisha would be helping with everything PR related—and all the final stages needed to be reviewed by me before Apocalypse Summit was officially ready. Then we had two weeks of production... there were already thousands of preorders...

"Well there's no point worrying about it now," she stated resolutely. She nudged my plate closer to me, indicating that I should eat. "You can't do anything about it until tomorrow at the earliest, so you should get some rest tonight. Or try to. And don't worry about the dishes or anything, I'll clean up before heading to bed."

I tried opening my mouth to protest, but Lacey talked over me. "I'm not arguing about it, Max—seriously."

Snapping my mouth shut, I looked at her closely. The way she crossed her arms and leaned forward, hair falling over her shoulders, legs tucked up under her.

When was the last time I had someone to come home and talk to? Vent to? It felt good, and already I could feel a weight lifted off my shoulders.

As if watching my daughter every day wasn't enough, she came to Cold Springs without a second thought, stepped back into my life, supported me, kept plates warm for me, and made me laugh.

What had I done all these years without her?

Something stirred in me, and I wondered if maybe Steven was right. Maybe there was still something there. More than the crush I'd been ignoring for so long.

But I'd given up on love a long time ago, thanks to Skylar. She'd lived here, in this penthouse, for a short time. Most days she was gone when I came home or irritated with the pregnancy and her body's changes. It had become clear quickly that we didn't make each other happy, not really. We didn't understand each other.

Lacey, though... she knew me in a completely different way. She knew me from the start; what really made me Max Munroe. Not the gaming mogul everyone saw, but the real me, under the layers of PR coaching.

If I went into my bedroom right now and tossed on a Guns N' Roses t-shirt, she wouldn't blink twice.

"I'll see you tomorrow morning?" she asked, pushing herself up from the island and grabbing her book. She rubbed at her eyes sleepily, glasses sideways, making me grin.

"Wait—" I said as she turned to leave.

She gave me a suspicious look over her shoulder. "If you ask me to get you a bowl of ice cream..."

My grin widened. "I can manage that myself, thanks. No, I was thinking... To thank you, I'd like to take you out for dinner sometime."

Lacey had always been an easy blusher. It was a trait she found embarrassing and I found endearing. The rosy color started at her collarbones and traveled up her neck, flushing her cheeks as she shook her head.

"Oh, no. You have way too much going on—"

"I insist," I said firmly, using my "boss" voice, as Steven liked to tease me about.

Her mouth snapped shut and she pressed her lips together, looking suddenly shy.

"Okay, but nothing crazy, alright? No fancy restaurants. I'd be fine with a food truck. You know how I feel about a good burger."

I laughed, feeling the rest of the day's stress melt away. "Don't worry, I have the perfect place in mind. It's my treat. I really owe you for everything. You've been a life saver, Lace."

Her blush deepened and I watched her gaze wander the room, looking anywhere but at me. "Rosie's wonderful, Max. You've done so well with her. And I think we had a bit of a breakthrough today. Although that might've been because I let her eat ice cream before dinner."

I gaped at her, then laughed again, unsurprised that she had stooped to such bargaining techniques.

"Well, whatever works. I'm just happy to see her getting more comfortable with you. And thanks for listening."

"Of course. Anytime. I mean it."

She sent me a soft smile and turned, heading toward the hallway and her bedroom.

I stayed leaning against the kitchen island for a few more moments, thinking about how my life had changed so dramatically over the years.

And how, now that Lacey was back in it, it felt like everything was in place.

Chapter 6

Lacey

"Oh my GOSH!" Kate McIntosh screamed, launching herself at me after walking into the burger and shake shack we'd agreed to meet at.

I laughed, catching her and glancing around to see the other patrons staring at us.

"I can't believe it," she gushed, pulling back and holding me at arm's length. "You're in Cold Springs! When Steven told me, I told him I needed proof. Honestly, Lace, I never thought you'd set foot in any city."

I scrunched my nose up, tugging her toward the little table I'd snagged in the corner. "Yeah... I never really saw myself as a city girl, but I kind of understand what the allure is now. Although I can't understand how anyone affords to live here."

"Tell me about it," she breathed, settling herself and slinging her purse over the back of her chair. "If it weren't for our combined income we'd definitely be living out in the suburbs and commuting. I love it here, though. All the hustle and bustle."

Out of all my old friends, Kate was the most energetic.

When we first met in eighth grade, I'd immediately disliked her. She was just *too* much. Too loud, too bouncy, too nosy. She'd been dragged to our lunch table by Amir, the kid assigned to show her around the school, and

I'd shot her an annoyed glance. I was trying to read a book, but I couldn't remember which...

After being shoved together for a few projects in our shared social studies class, it became obvious that we had a lot in common. We were like yin and yang, balancing each other out.

Where I was quiet, she was loud; where I tended to be more judgmental, she was a little bit compassionate. And like she'd pointed out—she preferred hustle and bustle and I preferred to be tucked away somewhere quiet.

But here we both were, in Cold Springs.

"It's so good to see you," I admitted, meaning it.

She made a face, sucking her teeth. "Mmhmm. Well, if you hadn't run off to college with that idiot..."

"Okay, okay." I held up my palms in surrender. "I know. You told me it was a bad choice then and I didn't listen. But you know how it is, live and learn."

"Still. You could've dodged that bullet."

I snorted. "True, but I still would've ended up at college. We would've been separated no matter what."

She shook her head, sadness settling on her features. "It wasn't just that though, was it? You didn't keep in touch after that, I'm sure because Craig didn't want you to." She sighed. "But there's no point rehashing the past. How have you been? And what are you doing *here*?" Her eyes narrowed. "Steven told me you came here for Max."

I opened my mouth to protest but couldn't find the words.

The problem was, Kate could read me like a book. She'd always been able to, and I was sure that hadn't changed in a decade or so.

"I didn't come here for Max," I replied, rolling my eyes. "I came here for his daughter..."

With a wince at her burst of laughter, I felt my face reddening.

Okay, maybe a small part of me had come here for Max. But so what? We were friends.

"Well, either way," Kate said, "I'm glad you're here and that Steven weaseled your number out of Max."

"Wait, what? What do you mean 'weaseled my number' out of him?"

"Oh, he didn't tell you? He walked in on Max on the phone with you. He said Max was all giggly—" I scoffed, unable to imagine him giggly "—and really beat around the bush before admitting you were here. As if we wouldn't find out eventually. We go to his place now and then for drinks, or out to eat."

"Yeah, he's mentioned you guys getting together a few times. I figured we'd run into each other eventually… I wonder why he didn't come right out and tell you I was here!"

She stared blankly at me for a moment, then busted out laughing again. I patiently waited for her to finish, trying not to blush at the looks we were getting from people.

"Would you care to explain yourself?" I mused.

"Lace," she huffed, arms spread out on the table as she lay half-across it. "You're kidding, right?"

I raised my eyebrows at her, shaking my head. She rolled her eyes.

"Obviously, he wanted to keep you all to himself as long as he could. No surprise there since that's been his MO since day one."

Now I did blush, sitting back in the chair and crossing my arms. I looked around a little desperately—where was the waitress?

"Kate, we've talked about this—"

"Exactly," she said in a flat voice, her humor immediately turning serious. "Lacey, it's been what—fifteen years at this point? You two are completely oblivious. He has had it bad for you since we were teenagers—"

As she continued the all-too-familiar rant, I tuned her out, focusing instead on the knot forming in my gut.

Kate, Steven and I were all friends throughout middle and high school. Kate and I had a ton of classes together, with Max and Steven interspersed here and there. We ate lunch together, spent the summers together bumming around town, and were practically inseparable... until my ex walked into the picture.

I remembered, roughly, the year Kate started giving Max curious glances. But she didn't actually say anything until we were sixteen and facing our first prom. Our conversation floated back to me as if it were yesterday:

"Has Steven seen the dress yet?" I asked.

"No way! He knows it's pink but that's it. I want it to be a surprise. Speaking of... did you pick one out yet?"

"I don't even know if I'm going to go. What's the point? We'll have a senior prom, too—"

"Wait, Max didn't ask you yet?"

A beat of silence. "Why would Max *ask me?"* At the time, I'd been truly dumbfounded.

"You're kidding, right? Have you not noticed the way he's always staring at you? Or trying to make you laugh? He has a crush on you, Lace."

I huffed out a laugh. "He does not."

"Psh, even Steven thinks so. We both thought he would have asked you by now..."

But he hadn't ever asked me to prom, which, at the time, seemed like a pretty clear sign that they were wrong. It was probably wishful thinking on their part, pairing up their two single friends.

Thankfully, the waitress showed up and Kate was forced to shut up long enough for us to place an order. The young girl returned quickly with our drinks, and I wrapped my hands gratefully around the coffee, knowing I'd need an extra boost of energy.

She pressed her lips together and gave me a meaningful look, one that I knew meant trouble.

"I'm not surprised that you somehow *still* haven't caught on, but you can't deny *your* feelings for him. Right?"

I stuttered, for some reason surprised that she'd dived right back into the conversation. She was blunt, and over the years I'd learned to appreciate it, but when it caught me off guard it could be jarring.

Especially when she was right. She was so right....

"What?" she asked with a smile, "You nervous he's going to figure it out and then you'll be unable to ignore your feelings in such close quarters? I mean, it's practically a rom com, Lacey. You two living together."

"So you do know why I'm here!" I exclaimed, trying to turn the conversation.

She rolled her eyes. "Steven mentioned that you're filling in until he can find another nanny. And that's great, really, although..." she eyed me suspiciously, "at some point you'll have to explain how exactly you made that work."

Guilt gnawed at me. But really, no one in my life knew that I'd lost my job. My mom thought I was taking some much-needed time off and I didn't have any close friends back home so there was no one to rant to about my sudden joblessness.

"Anyway," she continued, smiling gratefully at our waitress as the food arrived, "honestly, I think this is perfect. You two will finally have to own up to your feelings. There's no way you can see each other day in and day out and not act on all that repressed lust."

I scrunched my nose up, not liking my childhood crush being painted as a cheesy romance.

"I doubt that'll happen," I muttered, poking around at the chicken salad I'd ordered. "I spend way more time with Rosie than Max. Sometimes I'm already in bed by the time he gets home."

"Your bed, or his?" she asked with a lifted brow, and I rolled my eyes.

"Really though," she smiled apologetically, "sad to say, that sounds spot on for him. Steven and I have told him over the last few years that he needs to take a step back. Just because he owns the company doesn't mean he can't delegate. He has all those people working under him and it sounds like he's not seeing Rosie as much as he should."

She snuck a glance at me, and I took a deep breath, shaking my head.

"No. I mean, don't get me wrong, he's a great dad." I couldn't help the small smile curling my lips. "But yeah... he could be home more. Rosie really misses him when he's away."

She sighed. "Well hopefully when this new game is released, he'll relax a bit."

I put my fork down, facing Kate with an expression that told her what was coming was serious.

"Listen, I know you like to joke around about my crush, but —can you please not mention it? He is super stressed at work. I'm sure Steven's told you a little bit about what's going on, and I don't think he needs any other drama to worry about."

She pursed her lips, but dug into her food, muttering, "You two being helplessly in love with each other isn't 'drama' at this point. It's old news."

But she agreed to let sleeping dogs lie. For now, at least, the only one I needed to worry about was myself.

It wouldn't be *that* hard to ignore my errant crush on Max Munroe. I'd done it for years now. What was another few months?

Out on the street, the sun was streaming golden through the buildings, halfway to twilight. I was walking quickly, needing to get back to Skyside where Rosie would get dropped off by the bus. She had homework to do but then we'd decided to explore some of the parks nearby. Designating the eight-year-old my personal tour guide had sparked some pride and excitement in her, and it would get us outside for once.

Kate was accompanying me to say hi to Rosie before she met with a potential client. She was an interior designer and had built up her company diligently over the last decade, although she'd admitted as we chatted that this was the first year she felt financially stable.

A glimpse of color in a shop window caught my eye and I almost stumbled. She caught my elbow.

"Woah there. You good?"

"Yeah," I said, distracted as I took in the square-neck dress draped over a mannequin in the window. "Sorry. I think I need to go shopping soon. All my clothes are raggedy compared to the fashion standards in Cold Springs."

She laughed, looking every inch the businesswoman in her tailored pantsuit.

"We can make a date of it if you want, maybe sometime next week? Are you shopping for comfort, or an occasion?"

As we continued down the street, I felt my cheeks burn in a blush and silently cursed how reactive my body could be to stress. Kate hummed in curiosity, recognizing a tasty tidbit when she saw it.

"It's not a big deal," I muttered, giving her a look of warning, "but he wants to take me out to dinner. *To thank me*," I rushed on, trying to cut her off as she opened her mouth, "for coming to Cold Springs and helping out!"

She chuckled, responding darkly, "And I'm sure he'll love *helping you out* of whatever dress we find for you. Don't worry, we'll get something that'll have him confessing his undying love to you by the end of the night."

I groaned, already regretting telling Kate *anything*.

"Wait!" she exclaimed, stopping dead on the sidewalk and ignoring the glares of the people streaming by. "There!"

She grabbed my arm and practically dragged me across the street. I scanned the shops, wondering what the heck she was doing, but then I saw it.

"No way," I said, trying to pull away, but she had a few inches and a lot more muscle on her. She practically dragged me into a shop called The Factory.

"Hi," Kate said loudly and demandingly, approaching the first sales associate she saw, "we'd like to see the dress in the window—the floral one, please."

I turned in confusion, trying to spot the one she was talking about. My eyes widened as the saleswoman smiled tightly and headed in that direction.

"No way. I told him I didn't want to go anywhere fancy."

"You think that's fancy?" she asked critically, eyeing me. "It's a halter dress, Lace. Chill out. And just try it on!"

There was no fighting her, so I sighed and went along with it as the saleswoman returned with the dress, handing it to Kate and indicating where the dressing rooms were at the back of the store.

I slipped into the room and shut the door behind me, taking a quick glance in the mirror. The light breeze outside had mussed up my hair, but my cheeks were a pretty pink. With another long sigh I stripped off my long-sleeve shirt and jeans, struggling out of the latter.

Bra, or no bra?

Since it was a halter dress, I was resigned to stripping the bra off, too. It took me a few moments to struggle into the dress, but the fabric was light and airy. Like a caress on my skin as I smoothed it over my thighs.

It reached just above my knees and flowed beautifully. The fabric was a dark navy blue with a gorgeous floral print, well-balanced so that it didn't overwhelm me. The top actually fit surprisingly well, hugging my chest and waist before flowing over my hips. I took a look in the mirror and was surprised to see how the navy made my eyes look dark and sultry.

Maybe Kate was right. If Max had even an ounce of interest in me, this might just get a rise out of him.

I bit my lip at the thought of his caramel eyes dragging over my body. How many nights—both in my youth and as a single woman—had I thought of him that way? Imagined what it would be like... letting the person who knew me best explore all of me...

"You done?" she called, exasperated.

I shook off my dangerous thoughts and took a deep breath, stepping out.

"Okay, that's perfect," Kate deadpanned, looking impressed. "It'll be a crime if you don't buy this dress Lace."

"I don't know. I don't exactly have a bankroll saved away."

"So what? Isn't he paying you?"

He was, but I felt awkward about it; he'd insisted on at least giving me a "stipend" to spend around Cold Springs. I'd agreed with the assumption that I'd spend it taking Rosie out or on groceries.

"He is, but..."

"And this dinner was his idea, so if he doesn't want you embarrassing him... you know the media still pays attention to him here and there, right? Especially with the new game coming out."

I smoothed my hands over the dress, debating internally. But she was right—if there was any chance that they'd pay attention to me accompanying Max in public, I couldn't be seen in one of my shabby librarian skirts and an old blouse.

"Alright," I relented, turning toward the dressing room. "Give me a second to change, I'll meet you up at the register."

Ten minutes later, I was handed a small paper bag with the dress wrapped in tissue paper. Had I ever bought anything wrapped in tissue paper? Definitely not. It felt expensive and so, so far out of my comfort zone. But a part of me was thrilled, too. Why not splurge on something nice for myself? I deserved it after the last few months of stress and the constant feeling of failure.

"Hey," she said, slowing down as we approached Skyside. We had maybe five minutes until the bus arrived, give or take. I stepped to the side with her, out of the way of the foot traffic.

"Mmm?"

"I know you asked me not to keep bringing this up, and I really won't after this, but I have to ask... why don't you at least make a move? Worst case scenario he lets you down easy. You know Max; he'd never laugh or be hurtful about it."

My heart pounded with anxiety thinking about it.

"Kate, it's... it's more complicated than that. He isn't just some guy, he's a close friend. If I said anything about my... *crush*, and he didn't feel even a little bit the same way, I'd lose a really good friend."

She shook her head, brows knit. "You don't know that, Lace. You might actually feel better getting it out there!"

"No," I insisted, "I do know. Really. The problem would be me, not him. You know how I am. I'd be crushed by embarrassment if he turned me down. And I definitely don't fit into his life here. He lives in a penthouse with its own elevator!"

She chuckled, hefting her purse on her shoulder. "His life might look glamorous, Lacey, but I promise, he's the same old Max. A bit of a goof and a good guy all around." She sighed. "But I get it. It's all pretty intimidating and, like I said, you've never been a city girl."

I smiled sadly. "That, and Max is probably swimming in gorgeous women. I'm surprised I haven't seen any lurking around."

She let out a full-blown Kate McIntosh laugh, practically falling over in her heels.

"What?" I asked, unable to suppress a grin. She returned it, giving me a sassy nudge.

"Trust me, he's not swimming in women. Actually, it seems like he spends most of his time running from them or hiding away. Steven tried to set him up on a blind date a few years ago and he came up with every excuse under the sun not to go."

I raised my eyebrows, a little surprised. Max had never been a smooth talker or a ladies' man when we were younger, but still. He was incredibly handsome, funny, kind, sweet. Add "rich" into the mix and it was easy to see why any woman would want him.

A rumbling sound made us both look up as Rosie's bus came down the street.

"Promise me," she said quickly, reaching out to grip my hand in solidarity, "that if the opportunity presents itself, you won't be totally blind to it."

I nodded and gave her a small smile, but I couldn't imagine a world in which Max Munroe fell for a quiet, simple girl like me when he was leading a life of excitement and luxury.

Chapter 7

Max

For the tenth time this morning I cursed my forgetfulness, giving Tara an apologetic smile.

"Of course, go to lunch and don't worry about it—I'll get back on track with signing off on everything before you return."

She didn't seem convinced but grabbed her lunch anyway and headed for the elevators. I had an hour to hope and pray that Lacey could come through and bring me the pile of paperwork I'd totally forgotten at home this morning.

My phone pinged and I picked it up.

I can be there in twenty.

I typed quickly, relief flooding my body. **I'll owe you another dinner for this Lace.**

Those three little dots appeared, then disappeared. Appeared again... then stopped.

Uh oh. Had I scared her off?

"I'm an idiot," I groaned, leaning back and closing my eyes tightly.

"I won't argue with that."

Steven stood in the doorway of my office, looking tired. He'd had a tough few days of working with our IT team and legal to try and track down whoever leaked the shot of *Apocalypse Summit* ahead of the release.

Unfortunately, they hadn't been able to tie it to anyone. There were over eighty people who'd touched that one scene alone.

He dropped into a chair across from me. "Hope your day is going better than mine."

"I doubt it is," I said, then met his eye. "Is it completely insane that we're still doing this? Should I have sold the company years ago when offers started coming in?"

Steven's head tipped back and forth as he considered. "As your financial advisor, I'd say no; the company is worth way more now than it was then. But if you want out we should sit down and talk about what offers you'd accept. And as your friend, I'd also say no." He leaned forward, a grim smile on his face. "You love what you do, Max. No way around it. You created this empire out of passion and somehow, a decade later, you still want to be knee-deep in it. More power to you, but don't be surprised if I retire early."

He was only half-joking. But really, I didn't blame him. There were days I seriously considered making my exit.

While the first few years of building Journey Studios had been a whirlwind of brainstorming, creativity, and growth, lately I'd begun to feel like it was a little soul-sucking. When was the last time I'd spent the whole day with Rosie? Or had an entire weekend off? How many times was I going to have to see fake headlines about my private life, which was almost impossible to keep private these days no matter how boring I was?

When I thought back to the early days, when life was simple and my biggest concern was trying to find a cheap apartment just outside the city, it was tempting to walk away.

But I had close to two hundred employees cranking away, dependent on me for a steady income and security. Plus, some of them truly cared about game design the way I had once.

Had?

I got lost in thought; did I not care anymore? Was I finally burned out?

"Brace yourself," I said, knowing that if I didn't tell him that Lace was showing up, he'd never let me live it down. They'd both already berated me for keeping her a secret from them. "Lacey's coming in to drop off some paperwork I forgot at home this morning."

He stared at me. "That's convenient," he said vaguely.

"What's that supposed to mean?"

"When was the last time you forgot paperwork at home? Are you sure this isn't an excuse to see her more often?"

I clenched my jaw. My dentist was going to kill me if I kept this up. "No, dude. I've been super forgetful lately and walked out the door without it."

"Well when can we expect her?"

I glanced at my computer screen. "Probably within the next few minutes. Would you mind meeting her in the lobby? I'm trying to finish up a few other things here."

"Sure," he said breezily, standing with renewed energy. "You just stay right there behind your big, impressive desk, waiting for someone to escort her in."

I took a deep, calming breath, shaking my head as he headed out and towards the elevators.

Maybe a little, tiny part of me was anxious about having Lacey here. She obviously knew what I did. But she'd never seen Journey Studios. I gazed out across the floor. Did the navy blue, black and teal design look childish? Were the standing desks too much? I didn't want to look like I was trying too hard.

What are you doing? I berated myself, rubbing a hand over my face. *You built this place years ago, not a month ago in anticipation of her visiting. Besides, Lacey is the last person on earth who would judge you for paint colors.*

It was a long five minutes as I waited for Steven to return with Lacey in tow. The elevators opened and closed a total of four times, each ding of the bell making me stiffen in anticipation.

Finally, the door whooshed open, and I saw them. Steven was chatting animatedly, looking oddly boyish in his tan suit. She was smiling up at him and nodding along. In her arms was the stack of folders, clutched tightly to her chest. She wore a simple skirt and blouse with flats, but somehow still managed to outshine the much younger women on the floor as she stepped out of the elevator and followed Steven to my office.

"Hey," I said awkwardly, standing and immediately not knowing what to do with myself.

Lacey quirked a smile in return. "Hey yourself. These are what you wanted, right?" She held the hefty stack out with two hands and I took it solemnly, knowing that Tara would have a heart attack if I didn't get them signed before she returned. Luckily I'd gone through this process enough times that I could get away with scanning the documents instead of reading every single page.

"Yeah, thanks."

Steven interrupted, bouncing on the balls of his feet. "Hey, while she's here, why don't you give her a tour?"

I shot him a quick glare, but Lacey turned to me with excited energy. "You're probably busy," she said, but there was a hint of hope behind her words. I shrugged.

"Not really." *That* was a lie. "I can give you a quick walk around, if you really want to see it."

Steven was rolling his eyes behind her back. I ignored him, coming around the desk and gesturing for her to follow me. We were on the fourth floor of the building.

"Obviously this is my office… and this is where the first- and second-year designers, and sometimes interns, work." I indicated the open floor before us, an amalgam of different working styles and levels of anxiety.

Lacey looked at me quickly.

"What?" I asked.

"I'm surprised you don't surround yourself with your senior staff, I guess," she replied, gazing around us.

"Oh, yeah. Well I thought I could be of more help to those newer to the game." Pun intended. "You know, check in or have an open-door policy if they have any questions."

Her smile was filled with warmth, and I scratched the back of my neck, leading her out into the hallway. "You saw the lobby, I guess. Nothing too exciting there. This is a conference room where we have most of our meetings. And this is a meditation, or zen room. Just a room for people to chill really."

I opened the opaque glass door onto a decent-sized room painted light blue. Low, ambient music played in the background. There were plush chairs or meditation cushions for those who wanted to meditate. An impressive wall of plants was directly opposite us.

She looked floored. "This is amazing," she half-breathed. "I had an idea for something like this at the library, but no one could see the point of it."

As she turned to me, a voice interrupted us.

"Library, huh? You've definitely got the classic librarian look down."

I looked over her shoulder to find Victor eyeing her up and down as Lacey turned. She flushed and took a step back, shoulders bumping into my chest. Instinctively, I caught her upper arms.

"This is Victor," I said icily. "He's one of my lead designers."

Victor gave me a tight smile. In reality, he was my *only* lead designer and oversaw all other designers no matter their background or expertise.

Despite our rocky working relationship, he was one of the best in the industry. I was lucky to have him, even if I didn't particularly like him.

But I didn't like the way he was looking at her.

"Hi, I'm Lacey," she said, taking Victor's hand when he held it out. I watched as his thumb brushed across her knuckles. She pulled her hand back as if she'd been shocked. It took everything in me not to take her by the shoulders and maneuver her behind me, growling at Victor to back off.

"Lacey is a good friend," I said, staring Victor down. He looked momentarily surprised. Maybe because there was a hint of a threat in my tone. I was a pretty easygoing boss and didn't get riled up often. She noticed it and looked up at me over her shoulder. The shift in position made her ass graze my hip.

With a small cough, I placed a hand on her hip. Victor noticed immediately. A smile curled his lips as his eyes darted from my hand to our faces.

"Well it's nice to meet your friend," he purred, turning his full attention to her. "Hopefully we'll be seeing you around here more often, Lacey."

Lacey smiled weakly. She didn't seem in a rush to remove my hand, so I kept it there until Victor excused himself with a nod. Then she half-turned toward me, keeping the space between us tight despite the fact that we were now alone.

For a brief moment, blood rushed in my ears. She was looking up at me through her lashes and I wanted nothing more than to lean down and capture her lips with mine.

"Will you be home in time for dinner?" she asked hopefully, a hint of nerves still in her words.

I blinked, the sudden desire I'd felt a moment ago tempered by the thought of how much I still needed to get done today.

"Yeah, I should be. I have a few loose ends to tie up here but nothing too crazy. You really saved my ass bringing in those papers."

Her smile this time was genuine, more confident as she stepped back. "Okay, good. Well, I should probably get going so you can actually get some work done."

Suddenly I realized that the last thing I wanted was for her to leave.

All my life, I'd truly enjoyed my work. It was part of what made the long hours bearable; I loved what I did. But now... now I wanted to be home. With my daughter, with Lacey, laughing and chatting and chasing each other around the apartment.

"Alright," I replied, trying to keep my tone even and professional. "Let me walk you out."

"Oh, I'm sure I could find my way—" she insisted, but I had some bad news to break, and escorted her toward the elevators despite her protests. Eyes watched us as we crossed the open work floor. Probably wondering what I was doing with a female guest. My love life, or lack thereof, was a hot topic not only in the media but also at Journey, unfortunately. Lacey was the first woman other than Skylar to set foot on the grounds without business purposes.

Although technically, she'd brought me work papers.

"Hey, listen," I said once the elevator doors shut and it was just the two of us. "I have to adjust some things in my schedule, so I'm thinking we need to postpone the restaurant a bit."

Lacey's eyes widened. "That's fine, Max, really. You don't need to take me out at all—"

"No," I said firmly, watching her mouth snap shut and a flush color her neck. What was that about...? "No, I'm definitely taking you out. I don't want you to think I forgot. Let me take care of things here, and we'll figure out a good night, alright?"

She nodded, chewing on her bottom lip. A bad habit from when we were kids. Unthinkingly, I reached out and thumbed her lip from between her teeth. Her mouth parted and she stared up at me. The soft skin of her bottom lip was warm beneath my thumb, and for the second time today I had the urge to sway forward and kiss her.

The elevator dinged and I pulled my hand back like it was on fire. She took a deep breath, then stepped back.

Outside in the lobby employees came and went. Tara saw us as she entered the building and her eyebrows knit in confusion. I'm sure she was wondering who was taking up my time on a day I really needed to focus on work.

"I'll see you at home," I promised, walking Lacey out onto the sidewalk.

She didn't reply, only nodded, looking dazed. I went in for a hug just as she pressed up onto the balls of her feet, moving to kiss my cheek. In the awkward misunderstanding of the moment, I caught her quickly around the waist and her mouth dragged across my jaw, lips catching briefly on mine.

It was the lightest of touches, but it lit a fire in me. It didn't matter that we were standing outside where anyone could see us.

Right then, all I wanted was to drag her up to my office. Her hands clutched at my shirt and she pressed tightly against me, our eyes meeting with an intensity that I was sure meant she was feeling the same thing I was.

Right then, the Land Rover pulled up smoothly to the curve. Through the reflections glancing off the windshield I could see Gerald's raised brows.

Lacey let go of me quickly and I released her from the circle of my arms, praying that there wasn't an obvious sign of how badly I wanted her in that moment. I didn't need the paparazzi hiding around the corner to snap a picture of me half-hard for Lacey Weaver in the street.

"See you at home," she said, stepping toward the car with a smile. I waited until she slipped inside, then turned back toward my building.

Hopefully seeing this part of my world—the craziness that was Journey Studios and me trying to spearhead a company of this size—wasn't too off-putting. A part of me hoped that, after all was said and done, she'd stay close.

Maybe not in Cold Springs... but close.

By 5 p.m. I was relieved to see everything was almost done. This would be the first time in a long time I was leaving the office this early.

With a sigh, I set the stack of papers aside for Tara to grab on her way out. The office was almost empty, with just two designers hurrying to tidy up their desks and head out. Outside the sun was low behind the buildings, a false sunset.

"Have a good night," Tara called, grabbing the stack out of the bin and jogging down the hall. She'd get everything to Aisha for the final marketing push. We were nearing the big release, but I was still uneasy. If someone had managed to leak an old frame of the game, it made me think they were liable to leak more.

With a sigh I stood and headed for the breakroom, wanting to grab my jacket. Nights were getting cooler in the city.

Just outside the door, I paused, hearing two familiar voices in conversation.

"—what she's doing with a guy like Max. Of all the days you chose to go out to lunch! You really missed out."

That was Victor. I clenched my fists, knowing exactly what—or who—he was talking about.

"I don't know," the other voice sighed. His assistant, Jake.

Jake was also an intern and pretty young. Still in college, but according to Victor he did a good job. He had that roll-your-eyes-and-sigh personality going on, which I didn't find endearing.

"The tacos were worth it."

"Nah," Victor disagreed, and I could imagine his smirk; the way he was probably leaning against the counter with that ridiculous cardigan buttoned up over a long sleeve shirt. "You missed out, man. It's not every day you see a hot librarian."

Anger ran through my body like fire. It took everything in me at that moment to close my eyes and take a deep, calming breath. Before he could say anything else, I abruptly pushed open the door and strode in.

Victor faltered for a moment, and he straightened up.

Good. I wanted to have that effect on him. Maybe I'd been relaxed around him for too long, wanting to appear unbothered.

But today he was pushing the boundaries too far.

"Jake," I greeted, not even glancing at the young man. "Victor. I'm surprised you two are still here."

Victor smiled awkwardly, not meeting my eyes. "I'm surprised you're heading out early, Max. Big plans for the evening?"

"Yes; Lacey made dinner, and I need to get home to her."

I stared him down, my gaze boring into him to drive the point home. *She's mine.*

She's not, though, a small voice in the back of my mind reminded me. I ignored it.

After a moment Victor looked away uncomfortably. Reaching behind him, I sprung open the locker and grabbed my jacket. Victor flinched.

"I'll see you both tomorrow," I said flatly, turning and making my way to the door.

As I rode the elevator down to the lobby, Victor's words rang in my head: *It's not every day you see a hot librarian.*

It wasn't that I was blind to Lacey's attractiveness. In fact, you could argue that I'd been all too aware of it for a very, *very* long time.

The summer we turned fifteen was like an awakening. I don't know why, but suddenly I noticed things about her. The curve of her upper lip. Her lashes when she looked down shyly. And it was impossible to ignore the way she'd blossomed that year, of course... the subtle curves beneath her t-shirts and jeans.

How had I survived that summer? We spent weekends swimming at the town pool, Kate, Steven and I, and every time I died inside a little more knowing I couldn't have her. She'd never shown any interest in me other than wanting to be close friends.

And now she was a woman, and even more gorgeous.

If anyone was unaware of it, it was Lacey herself.

Already I'd caught a few other tenants in Skyside shooting her interested glances when we went out in the morning, Lacey chatting with Rosie about school and their plans for later in the day as I followed a few feet behind. The way her hair caught the light and her laughter, it turned heads. She just never noticed.

Victor would be an idiot if he wasn't attracted to her, but that didn't mean I had to be happy about it.

As I strode toward my car, I thought of a parallel universe where, for some reason, Lacey fell for his fake charms. Just the thought of his hands on her, as he leaned in to close the distance between them...

I rolled my shoulders and cracked my neck. Just a short ten-minute drive home and I'd see her again and reassure myself that she'd never, ever be his.

I wouldn't allow it.

Navigating the city streets, I thought about how Lacey truly did embody the cliché of a "hot librarian." When we were kids it seemed odd that she wanted to be a librarian, but now it made sense. She was perfect for it. Good with Rosie, too, even if my daughter was still a little unsure of her.

Plus, she was smart. Sharp, actually, and she was good at reading people. There was still an air of shyness around her as an adult. She was reserved, quiet. If I closed my eyes I could picture her perched behind a desk, a book open in her lap.

The thought calmed me enough that as I pulled into the parking garage, anger was no longer my main emotion.

"Hello, Mr. Munroe," Becca, one of the regular receptionists, greeted. I gave her a polite smile and nod.

"Good afternoon, Becca."

In the lobby I passed a guy from the 7th floor who I'd seen eye Lacey from afar. He was good-looking, maybe a few years younger than us.

My mind started going to that dark place again, imagining her pressed up against someone else's body, and I shook the thought off. Instead, I focused on a question that had been bugging me for a while: how had Lacey managed to get two months off of work?

From what I'd gathered from our conversations, she was pretty high up on the totem pole at the local library she worked at. It was a decent size, in a town of just under 35,000 and with a staff of about 20 that she oversaw.

She'd been here for two weeks now, and I hadn't even asked. What a bad friend I was, staying so busy I didn't have time to clarify her work situation. I knew how much I appreciated that she'd been able to take time off to help me out.

My phone vibrated as the elevator hauled itself slowly upwards. Steven's name appeared on the screen, with the message: **Heard Vic met Lacey today. Running his mouth as usual.**

My jaw clenched as I thumbed open the screen and typed a quick reply.

If he knows what's good for him he'll stay away. But I don't think she'll have to come to the office often anyway.

Sounds like you're staking a claim, buddy.

I could practically hear the amusement in his voice.

No, I typed back, **just keeping her safe from that loser. You can't tell me you wouldn't do the same.**

The three dots appeared, then disappeared. After a moment, his solemn reply came: **True, but if you're not careful, some other rich handsome guy in Cold Springs will snap her up. Brace yourself.**

With a sigh, I knocked my head against the wall and tucked my phone away.

He wasn't wrong. There was definitely a possibility that, while she was here, Lacey would meet someone. Especially since she had all day to wander around town and run into single guys. It's not like I had any free time to spend with her, so I couldn't blame her for seeking out companionship.

All it would take was bumping into some charming guy on a street corner, an offer of coffee, maybe dinner later...

The elevator dinged and the doors opened into the foyer. I stepped out and walked purposefully down the hall toward my door, excited to see both my girls. Dammit, I thought to myself, there I go again.

Steven's warning was a bitter reminder of everything I couldn't have. But I had to keep telling myself over and over: it was better to have Lacey here, even if she's not mine.

We were making up for lost time, and I wouldn't ruin it by acting on a schoolyard crush.

Chapter 8

Lacey

Early Saturday afternoon saw Rosie and I getting ready to go out and explore Mabel Humphrey Library. It was well known for its size and quality of books, and I was curious to get a look. Rosie needed a book for a report, and I'd offered to help her find one.

Max was off doing an interview, one I had every intention of checking out on YouTube later—in secret. He'd been embarrassed when I asked what he was up to today, but Rosie and I were both excited for him. Too bad I couldn't get away with watching it Live.

"Almost ready?" I called, hearing the *tap tap* of Rosie's feet as she ran around her room trying to find her favorite red jacket.

She yelled back something unintelligible, and I chuckled.

I'd spent a fair amount of time around kids when I was at Pratt, especially in my first few years when I was the children's librarian. But having so much one-on-one time with Max's daughter was wonderful.

At first, I'd been nervous, not sure she would accept me. Rosie was coming around slowly, though.

There was a knock at the door. We weren't expecting anyone, and I wondered who it was.

Max had assured me that only a few people had cards to the penthouse elevator, so…was this maintenance? Or some other staff member coming up to give me info about something?

I started walking toward the door, but to my surprise, it opened before I got there.

Frozen, I stared as a long-legged woman stepped in and closed it behind her, shaking out her curly locks.

Skylar West.

She turned, her striking light eyes looking me over. She didn't seem surprised to see me. Had Max told her about me? My stomach twisted with nerves at the possibility, but then, why wouldn't he? I was watching *their* daughter, after all.

"Hi," I said numbly. "I'm Lacey."

"I know," she replied, walking toward me. Even a casual saunter looked like she was heading down a runway, ready to stun the crowd.

Skylar barely looked at me. She breezed right past, heading for the hallway.

Obviously, she knew where Rosie's room was.

"Honey," she called, her voice throaty and full, "mommy's home!"

My heart stuttered at the words. Home? Did Skylar think of this—Max's place—as home? He'd told me she was almost never here, and Rosie had pretty much confirmed that.

The eight-year-old appeared in the hallway, her eyes wide and her hand was clutching that red jacket. But she wasn't smiling. Her gaze moved from Skylar to me quickly, and I smiled reassuringly.

"Hi darling," Skylar gushed, kneeling to pull Rosie into a hug. Rosie hugged her back, and it seemed genuine. So maybe she was initially shocked to see her mom.

"Mom, what're you doing here?" Rosie asked, a small mirror-image of the model, but with Max's caramel eyes. "Daddy didn't say you were coming—"

Skylar laughed. "I know, honey, I wasn't planning on it but I had an opening in my schedule, so I wanted to see you. Now, how do you feel about getting some breakfast and going shopping?"

I didn't mention that it was a few hours past breakfast at this point, or that Rosie had already had several pancakes. Instead I watched, leaning up against the wall, as Rosie worked at a smile.

"Okay," she said, glancing at me quickly. "I was going to go to the library with Lacey, but..."

"Your mom can take you," I was quick to chime in, not wanting to step on anyone's toes. It was odd that Skylar had just shown up here, but she had more of a right to be here than I did. She was Rosie's mother after all. Skylar glanced over her shoulder at me.

"She needs a book," I explained, "for a report at school."

Skylar didn't seem thrilled with the suggestion, but she stood and took the jacket from Rosie, helping her into it.

"Okay. We can make a stop at the library, too. I wanted to buy you new boots. It'll be winter in a few months."

Ah, so *this* was how Rosie's closet had become packed to the brim. I bit my lip, aware that Rosie already had several pairs of boots and really didn't need any more.

"You don't mind, do you, Lacey?" Skylar asked breezily, passing me with Rosie's hand in hers. "I'm sure you need to clean the house, or... something."

My mouth parted and I turned, taking a faltering step as they reached the door. Skylar swept it open and gave Rosie a gentle nudge into the foyer. The elevator doors were already open.

They were gone before I could get out a response. Despite being alone now, my face reddened in embarrassment and I crossed my arms.

Clean the house "or something"?

I mean, she wasn't wrong. I did clean the house here and there, but not often. He had an actual housekeeper that came twice a week when Rosie was at school and he was at work. We'd run into each other a few times—Monica. She was really sweet and did an amazing job.

With a pout, I turned back to the apartment and stalked to my room, intent on going out anyway.

Then guilt overtook me as I saw my open laptop, left on my nightstand from the night before.

I should really job search…

Not that I wasn't enjoying my time with Rosie, but when this all ended I needed something to go back to. Actually, there were a few other things I should get done, too, like giving my mom a call to check in and explain where I was.

She'd be thrilled that I was with Max; I could practically hear her ranting about him already. He was a fixture at my house during most of high school. She always thought of him as a son, even though she'd only set eyes on him in magazines since we all went our separate ways.

Mom actually lived only a few hours away from Cold Springs, in a small one-story house she bought after dad passed. She had some good friends who had moved there, and they encouraged her to relocate as well. She was always trying to get me to move closer to her, but I was comfortable on the east coast. I hadn't had a reason to leave until… well, until a few months ago.

With a sigh, I kicked off my flats and resigned myself to staying in. It was just a matter of where to start first—confess my whereabouts to my mother, or make plans for a future I couldn't imagine?

It was freshman year of college. Kate was visiting the campus and we were crammed into my dorm room. Luckily my roommate, a girl I couldn't quite connect with, spent almost every night with her boyfriend at his dorm. We were watching a movie and eating through a bag of chocolate.

"*You should see Max,*" *she gushed, an impressed look on her face.* "*He actually took Steven's advice and found a public relations contractor to give him a... a makeover, I guess.*"

I scrunched my nose, not liking the idea of Max needing to be made over. *What was wrong with him the way he was? His face flashed through my mind: that lopsided grin, those sun-kissed eyes and dark hair curling where it reached his ears...*

"*Hellooooo,*" *she drawled, snapping a finger in front of my face. Her eyebrows were raised, and I gave her a light shove away.*

"*Don't,*" *I warned, knowing where this was going.*

My cell phone chimed from somewhere in the pile of comforters we were nested in. Digging around for it, I was happy to have an excuse to hide my blush from Kate.

She'd known about my crush on Max for years now, but what did it matter? We were literally thousands of miles away and his company was taking off in a big way. If what I heard secondhand from Kate was true, investors were climbing over each other to get a piece of his start-up.

My face fell when I finally found the phone and saw the name on the screen.

Why had part of me expected it to be Max? As if he could feel me thinking about him all the way out west... if he could read my mind, he would've cut me loose sooner. Been weirded out by the turn my private thoughts often took when we were alone, which wasn't often now thanks to—

Craig. *My phone chimed again, another text from my boyfriend coming in. I didn't need to look at her face to know what expression was on it. She didn't like Craig; no one did, really. Mom never asked if he was coming when I visited and, instinctually, I never offered to bring him.*

A warm hand wrapped around my ankle. My gaze snapped to Kate; she was right next to me. So who...?

The dream fractured as I became conscious of my actual surroundings. I jerked my knee up, a gasp on my lips as I stared wildly at the man in front of me.

Max.

But not teenage Max; no, this version of my friend was a grown man. While *cute* would have been a word I used to describe him in high school, now a different one was whispered by that traitorous voice in the back of my head: *enticing*.

A blush colored my cheeks. The dream hadn't left the room completely and my blood was still rushing with longing.

He had wrapped a hand around my ankle and was gently shaking it to wake me. He gave me an apologetic grin.

"Sorry—you okay? You were snoozing hard."

I eased myself up and put together where I was: on his couch, in Cold Springs. It had been *years* since that night in college.

Unfortunately, as I took stock of myself mentally and emotionally, it was obvious that my feelings hadn't changed much over that period of time. He still made me nervous in a delicious way, especially when I was caught off guard like this.

My eyes darted to the laptop on the coffee table. 1 p.m.?

"What are you doing here?" I asked.

Then my brain caught up with my body and I leaned forward, almost falling off the couch to shut my laptop quickly. Had he gotten a glimpse of the job search? He was still wearing his jacket and carrying his work bag, so maybe not.

His brows creased. "I got off work early. I was thinking we could all go out to dinner tonight—I know I owe you a one-on-one meal but there's this hot dog place Rosie loves. Wait until you hear what it's called—"

He straightened up and looked around the apartment. He suddenly realized how quiet it was.

"Where is she?"

Tucking my legs under myself, I gave him a strained smile.

"Skylar showed up a few hours ago and took her out. Shopping, I think, but they're stopping by the library too."

His face fell. He suddenly looked exhausted, the skin under his eyes puffy, a permanent frown settling on his brow.

"Ah... I didn't know she was coming to town. It would have been nice to get a text."

"I figured. Rosie seemed happy to see her, and I wasn't sure... well I wasn't really comfortable..."

He dropped to the couch, his eyes wide. "Don't worry about that. I would never expect you to step in. This stuff... it's between me and Skylar. Technically she's allowed to swing by and take Rosie out. But still, she should've texted to give me a heads up. She doesn't usually just show up like this." Confusion flashed across his face.

But that little voice in my head came up with a reason Skylar might've paid a surprise visit—if she had even a vague idea of who I was to Max, and knew that I was here...

I bit my lip, not wanting to stir up any trouble.

"It's fine. She didn't mention dinner, so they'll probably return before then. Do you need to get any work done?"

I couldn't help the hopeful tilt to the question. He caught it and smiled, settling back into the couch even more, his work bag forgotten.

"Nope. I'm determined not to work tonight, actually. We are all crossing 't's and dotting 'i's at this point, so my part in the process is over. For now."

I looked at him and squinted, noticing something was a little off.

"Max, is that…" A chuckle escaped and I covered my mouth. "Do you have makeup on?"

He shot me an embarrassed look, rubbing at his face. I laughed louder at his poor attempts to remove the makeup.

"It looks good on you," I cooed, giving him a nudge. He nudged back and I lost my balance, overcorrecting and then falling into his lap. We were both laughing now, Max still attempting to rub off the remnants of his interview and me looking up at him with a happy grin.

He sighed deeply. It sounded both satisfied and sad, somehow.

"When I started this whole thing, no one told me I'd be wearing makeup," he confessed. "Or appearing on talk shows, or in tabloids." His face darkened. "With Skylar in town and the new game coming out I'm sure they'll come up with something. They'll claim we're back together, or that she's trying to steal Rosie from me."

I carefully pushed myself up into a sitting position, the mood growing heavy with the turn in conversation.

"Any time a woman like Skylar is involved, people can't help but speculate. Could she be any more gorgeous? If she's seen coming and going at Skyside it'd be hard to imagine you two didn't have something going on."

I was looking anywhere but at him, the bitter burn of jealousy reminding me once again that at least a small part of me wanted him to be more than a friend.

He snorted.

"Just because someone is outwardly pretty doesn't mean they're the same on the inside," he muttered. "Skylar and I had our time. It was fun at first, but that's all it was ever going to be. When things got serious…" He shook his head, eyes finding mine. The afternoon light reflected off of them, making them shine a copper that took my breath away.

"She's never been there for me the way I needed her to be."

I laughed uncomfortably, not really knowing what to say.

"Yeah, because that's what every guy is looking for in a woman. Support."

Leaning toward me and bumping my shoulder with his, he frowned. "We both know there's more to relationships than good looks." The dry way he said it made me wonder briefly what he thought of Craig. We'd never really spoken directly about my all-consuming relationship. But he continued on. "I mean, you're the full package, Lace. You're smart, funny, pretty and so supportive. Any guy would be lucky to have you."

I felt my cheeks heat at that last bit and looked away, but he reached out and put a hand on my knee. Even through my jeans, his touch seared.

"Hey, I'm serious. Skylar can't hold a candle to you."

I smiled because of how ridiculous that sounded.

"Max, come on. She's a *model—*"

"So?" he asked, brows knit as he sat straighter. "She's pretty in the right clothes, yeah, but not everyone is into that. It wasn't what drew my attention to her, at first."

"Oh?" I asked, turning to him with my full attention now. "You never told me about that. How you two met."

He shrugged. "Some big socialite party. I didn't know anyone there, and I didn't really want to be there, but my old PR rep was really pushing public appearances. I was wandering around a room full of rich people picking shrimp cocktail and fancy hors d'oeurves off of little plates, pretending I wasn't absolutely starving. And then I saw Skylar—she was in the kitchen, sitting on the counter in her cocktail dress, and she was spraying a can of whipped cream right in her mouth."

I almost choked at the image. Was he kidding? *Any* man would be attracted to that.

He shrugged. "There was just something about it. She wasn't doing it for show. She wasn't trying to fit in, or mingle, she was craving something sweet and went for it without a second thought. I don't know. I guess I was drawn to how she was so unapologetic about the things she wanted." He sighed. "For a long time, I thought we wanted each other. But Skylar didn't want to settle down, and when we tried to make it work it was obvious that we were both unhappy. Neither one of us wanted to raise a kid together and show them that the world is a miserable place, so…"

"So she went after what she wanted," I said quietly.

Skylar West had turned down a life with Max and her daughter.

It sounded absolutely crazy to me, but at the same time, I could kind of understand it. She was a strong woman and, as poorly as she'd treated me earlier with her upturned nose, I couldn't hate her. Partly because I trusted him, and if he was so convinced she wasn't that bad, then I'd give her a shot.

In the comfortable silence that followed, my body instinctively swayed toward Max, as if drawn by a thread. He leaned toward me as well, our shoulders brushing.

For a moment, it felt like something was building. His words echoed in my mind:

You're the full package, Lace.

Did he mean it, though? If that was true, could Max ever want me the way he'd once wanted Skylar?

I held my breath as he held my gaze and leaned ever closer, a determined look on his face.

And then the front door clicked open, Skylar's heels clicking down the hallway and Rosie singing out, "We're home!"

Chapter 9

Max

Three weeks until the release. *Only three more weeks.*

I'd been reminding myself of that fact all day. For at least an hour after lunch I'd searched flights and possible getaways. I wanted to bring Rosie somewhere after all this was over. Leave Journey in Victor's hands, maybe, with Steven keeping a close eye on him.

Just long enough to get away, recuperate.

If Lacey was up for it I could invite her, too, as another way to repay for helping out.

The image of her in a bathing suit flashed through my mind and I felt the beginning of arousal. I blinked as the TV screen flickered, scene changing.

The audio was off. Lacey and Rosie had both gone to bed hours ago. Rosie's school took a fieldtrip outside of the city to a place where they could see dinosaur footprints in stone. The nerd in me was jealous, and I know Lacey was impressed with the trip.

When we were Rosie's age our fieldtrips consisted of the local museum or the cranberry farm. Kids these days had it good.

My eyes felt tired and swollen. Tomorrow I'd look like hell, and Aisha would give me a hard time for it because we had a few more public appearances lined up. She was even trying to talk me into taking some young actress out for breakfast just to stir up some news, but I refused. That was the kind of attention I didn't want.

Clicking the TV off, I sat in the dark for a few moments, letting my thoughts slow to a trickle and my eyes adjust. It felt fabulous to sit here quietly with my thoughts.

Outside, blocks of light from the other apartment and office buildings peppered the dark sky. It was pretty, and up here the hush of traffic was a lull instead of annoying.

As my eyes were growing heavy from exhaustion finally setting in, a faint *click* further in the apartment caused me to shift. I closed my laptop and turned toward the hallway, where a subtle amber glow lit up Lacey's bare feet.

She walked the edge of the living area and yawned, rubbing at her eyes—her glasses were off so she couldn't see more than a few feet in front of her.

I held my breath, taking in what she was wearing.

Or... what she *wasn't* wearing.

Only half of her PJs from earlier remained; the top half, an oversized t-shirt that barely grazed the top of her thighs.

She padded into the kitchen, heading for the water jug and reaching up in the cabinet for a mug.

The shirt rose as well, revealing the lace edges of her pink underwear.

My desire for her was immediately lit like a match. If I'd doubted before that I still wanted her, that I was still attracted to her, the answer was quite clear right now.

I felt myself stiffening and reached down to touch myself, managing to keep quiet.

She poured water into the mug, took a deep drink, sighed contentedly, and headed back the way she'd come.

My eyes traveled up her legs, to that hem just brushing her thighs. I imagined my fingers slipping beneath it, ghosting over the silk of her panties. Hand gripping her hip the way it had in the office the other day—but this time, with less barriers between us. Less annoying interruptions.

The amber light in the hallway disappeared as her door clicked shut.

I let the breath I was holding out, trying to ignore the growing tent in my pants. Did I feel a little guilty about silently watching her move through the apartment in next to nothing?

Yes, but it was harmless.

I didn't have any intentions to act on my unrequited—and now literally restrained—desire for Lacey.

Even if we were going to be living together for at least a few more weeks.

I was sure I could control myself.

Chapter 10

Lacey

Kate and Steven have twin boys. I meet them when Kate had to bring them to lunch because their daycare was closed for the day courtesy of a lice outbreak.

The smaller of the two, Eli, sits in Kate's lap as she combs through his thin blonde hair with a frown.

I'm eyeing Evan, seated on my lap.

"I swear, if they got them..." she muttered. The boys are almost two and so far, well-behaved. Both quiet, gazing up at us here and there as they munch on the snacks Kate brought in her oversized bag.

"I thought you said you used the comb and couldn't find anything?" I asked nervously, shifting Evan into a position where I could get to the French onion soup in front of me. He scrunched up his little nose at the smell of it but I was practically drooling with hunger.

"I did but I'm nervous I missed something. Can you imagine the nightmare if they did get them?"

I shivered, not wanting to imagine. "Honestly, I don't know how you handle two."

"Plenty of people have two kids, Lace," she scoffed.

"That's not what I meant. Two that are *the same age*! It's great that they're so well-behaved though."

Evan gave me a cute little smile as our waiter finally returned, lugging two baby seats that he quickly strapped to the chairs. I gave him a grateful smile and shifted Evan over to the seat nearest me, buckling him in. She blew a raspberry on Eli's cheek before doing the same.

Now toddler-free, we turned our attention to lunch.

The boys chattered to each other in a language only they could understand, and I couldn't help smiling at their small arguments and the excitement when bite-sized chicken nuggets appeared on little plates. A part of me couldn't help wondering how I ended up where I was in life… didn't I dream of being a mother, once? Of settling down somewhere with a man who made me happy?

She talked about work, mostly, as we ate. She loved her job but some of her clients were insanely high-end and also insane. They had odd requests, and I laughed in bewilderment as she told me about one divorced CEO who asked her to procure a taxidermy alligator to be the centerpiece of his living room.

"Be happy Max isn't that kind of rich," she deadpanned as the waiter removed our empty plates and asked if he could get us anything else. We declined, both of us stuffed, the twins sleepily happy now that their bellies were full.

A comfortable silence, interrupted by the hushed sounds of the diners around us, settled. These were some of my favorite moments with Kate. She'd always been the loud one, but when she was quiet, it was easy and somehow comforting as well. Neither of us felt the need to fill the space between us with words.

My eyes trailed over our surroundings.

The restaurant we were in was casual, almost more of a coffee shop where the patrons relax and kick back. There were a few younger people around, possibly students, with laptops open and earbuds in. Over in the corner was a large velvet couch, coffee table, plants trailing along the front window, and—

She caught me staring at the pile of magazines on the nearby table. My eyes snapped away from it quickly.

The hint of bitterness I felt inside must have been showing on my face, because she reached out a comforting hand.

"Hey, is everything okay?"

With a deep sigh, I told her everything. Skylar showing up the other day, whisking Rosie off for a surprise shopping trip, and the awkward moment of her return.

"Wait," she said, sitting up straight. "So you two were having a 'moment' when she came back!?"

With a groan, I buried my face in my hands.

"I don't know… maybe? Or maybe it's just wishful thinking."

"Ha!" She pointed a finger at me, startling the twins with her outburst, a triumphant twinkle in her eyes. "So you admit it then? You've got a thing for Max!"

I rolled my eyes and pushed my glasses up my nose. "I really don't want to get too deep into it. Not after yesterday's fiasco. But… yeah. Maybe I have *a little bit of a thing* for him."

She was mid-happy dance when I interrupted her, reaching out to catch her excited punches and silence her squeal.

"It's probably nothing," I insisted, trying to convince myself as much as her. "Just a product of the situation, right? I mean, I've been single for a few years now and yeah, Max is objectively attractive—" I ignored Kate's snort—"and even in that huge penthouse it's kind of hard to avoid each other…"

She gave an irritated huff, picking Eli up since he'd started to fuss, and bouncing him in her lap.

"When are you two going to learn?" she asked, and the hard edge of annoyance in her voice actually caught me off guard. "This isn't new. You've never outright admitted it but you've *always* had a thing for Max. And if what you're telling me is true, it sounds like he was making his attraction to you *pretty* clear."

My gaze shifted toward the magazine.

Skylar West was on the cover, draped in fur.

"How am I supposed to compete with that?" I muttered.

She wrinkles her nose. "Skylar?" She scoffed, leaned over with a tight grip on Eli, and flipped the magazine over. The couple sitting on the velvet couch shot us suspicious looks.

"You have nothing to worry about with Skylar, trust me."

I realized then that I'd never really talked to Kate, or Steven, about Max's ex. They hadn't brought her up before. Maybe intentionally, since they were both so insistent on my feelings for him.

Curious, I decided to dive right in.

"Weren't they serious, though? I mean, they had Rosie together, and lived together. He told me as much."

She nodded, her demeanor now solemn as the toddler lulled sleepily on her shoulder. Evan was scrunched into the corner of his high chair, playing distractedly with the plastic spoon and plate in front of him.

"Yeah, they were serious. You know Max, though. He was going to be serious no matter what. I don't think Skylar was at first, but he was pretty devoted to her. I think she saw that and gave in. For a little bit, at least."

She sighed before bucking up and giving me the whole story.

"Steven and I weren't sure when he started bringing her around. And don't get me wrong, Skylar definitely lives a very different lifestyle than we've all chosen. But she came from practically nothing. Worked her butt off as a teenager to get where she is. I can respect that." She gave a half-hearted shrug. "That doesn't mean they were a good fit, though. Not for the long term at least."

I was silent for a few moments, comparing notes against what he's already told me. Not that I didn't trust him, but I wasn't sure if he'd glazed over some of the more important aspects of their relationship.

"So was he happy?"

Kate winced. "At first, yeah. He was riding a high though. Journey Studios was doing great, he'd just come out with his second game that won a few awards. And yeah, he snagged himself a beautiful woman that he enjoyed spending time with. But the longer they were together, Lace, the more obvious it became that they weren't a good match. I'm so happy he got Rosie out of it. But sometimes I wish he hadn't gotten involved with Skylar. I think it took a lot of the laughter out of him, you know? Even before the split, he just got quieter. And more serious. He didn't hang out as much with us." She shook her head. "Still doesn't, really."

A part of me felt guilty about asking. Maybe he didn't want me to know how tough the relationship was on him, and that's why we hadn't really talked about it.

But still, I felt a little better knowing, now, where everything stood.

Not just because I had a crush on Max, but because I wanted to make sure there was actually a place for me in his life. I didn't want to be stepping on any toes, making anyone uncomfortable—it looked like Rosie already had enough feelings to unravel when it came to her parents.

She didn't need me making it more complicated, and he didn't need me riling up his ex just by existing.

"But honestly, Lacey, from what Steven tells me Max has been doing a lot better now that you're here."

I couldn't help laughing, and when she gave me a little nudge under the table and asked "What?" defensively, I told her, "I don't know. I see him every day, when he can finally pry himself out of the office at least, and he seems miserable."

"Well...yeah, okay. You're right to an extent." She leaned in, dropping her voice to just above a whisper. "Listen, between you and me, I think he's close to getting out of the industry. Or maybe taking a step back, at least. It sounds like, from what Steven says, the last year or so hasn't been what Max wants when it comes to that work-life balance. He's not making games anymore. He's running a company. You and I both know that isn't why he started Journey."

As her words sank in, so did sadness.

I remembered the Max I used to know. The lanky teen who got excited over new video games coming out, could ramble on and on about how certain scenes or characters were designed, geeked out over certain books and movies.

I missed that Max.

And Kate was right; this whole time I'd been in Cold Springs, I hadn't seen any sign of that spark of excitement in him. Even with all the media outlets talking about *Apocalypse Summit* being his best work yet, he trudged into the apartment every day looking more and more dejected.

"It wouldn't be the worst thing," I murmured, thinking of Rosie.

She nodded. "And it's not as if he isn't set up for a brief, or even permanent, retirement," she said knowingly, her brows raising.

I didn't doubt it. He could sell Journey Studios, but even if he didn't and just took a step back, he'd still be raking it in.

"Anyway," she sighed, beginning to go through the motions of getting ready to head out, "if you're worried about Skylar, don't be. She makes an appearance now and then, but I doubt it's crossed his mind that he could casually sleep with her when she's in town. He's too much of a gentleman."

I bit my lip, thinking of a few times I'd seen that flash of darkness in him; that demanding voice that tolerated no questions...

"You should make a move."

There was a beat of silence as I processed her words, and then I couldn't help laughing.

The idea seemed ludicrous. I gave her an apologetic smile for laughing at her.

Since we were spilling secrets, maybe this was the time to tell her *everything*.

"Hey, I know you've been wondering how I managed to get out here for a few months," I started, helping collect the boys' odds and ends as she tucked things into their carry bag. Her glance was full of questions and curiosity, but she didn't interrupt. "My job back home is no longer. I was let go."

I felt my face heating with embarrassment as she slowly straightened up. Eli half-turned in her arms as if he was as confused as she was.

In the moment of silence, I felt my heart pounding in my chest. There were so many mixed emotions coursing through my veins: relief, shame, trepidation.

She pursed her lips together, looking me over carefully.

"Oh my gosh, what happened? I know you well enough to know you didn't drop the ball."

The sudden urge to tell her everything, every frustrating little detail about that job and the new director, flooded through me. My mouth opened, but I closed it quickly. I needed to keep myself in control. Taking a deep breath, I explained, "They hired a new director, a younger guy who immediately didn't like me. He shot down a bunch of my ideas for improving the library, and then he just cut me loose. Said my ideas didn't line up with where the library wanted to be, in the future."

The words came out dry and bitter. Kate looked appalled, her upper lip curled.

"Really?" she huffed. "So he was threatened, I'm guessing."

I nodded reluctantly. It was the same thing I'd been thinking every day since they let me go. And it was what some of my old coworkers had whispered as I packed up my office, or said over the phone later, apologetically.

"It seems like it, yeah. I don't think he liked how loyal the rest of the staff were to me, as the interim director. And when he came blazing in, he didn't make any friends."

She shook her head. "Well, you're better off. You'll find something else, Lace."

I hummed half-heartedly. "Towns out that way are small, Kate, and most people stay at their jobs for *decades*. Someone would literally have to die for an opening to come up out there."

She shrugged. "So don't go back."

In that moment, as Kate slung her bag over her shoulder and stood, it dawned on me that she was right.

Not going back was an option.

But if I didn't go back, where would I go instead?

I unbuckled Evan and picked him up, double-checked that we'd left a decent tip, and followed Kate out onto the street. Her SUV was parked a short distance away. As we walked, she looked over at me, her expression pensive.

"Lace, I know losing that job probably has you down. But listen, you're going to move onto bigger and better things. Life is funny that way."

We reached the car, and she opened the door, unloading the bag and buckling Eli in. She turned and took Evan from me, continuing to talk with a no-nonsense attitude.

"You've got to remember your roots. What got you there—and here—in the first place. You're brilliant. You're loyal. And you have amazing ideas.

"And, also, you're here, saving his ass. You know, you're a big part of why he has been so successful."

I frowned, giving her a look of disbelief. She propped a hand on her hip.

"You're the one who got him into reading, Lacey! It's pretty obvious that that's where he pulled his creativity and energy from. Still does, I'm guessing. He has that silly little room full of action figures."

The room I was currently sleeping in. I bit back a smile, warmth flooding through me at the memory of Max in his bedroom, feet kicked up on the desk as he devoured the *Lord of the Rings* series.

"Anyway," she said breezily, leaning in and giving me a tight hug. I didn't want to let her go. I was lucky to have her as a friend, wishing we'd done a better job of staying in touch before now. "You'll do fine wherever you end up next. It would be nice if it were here, though. Cold Springs is full of opportunity. Plus, we're not that far from your mom, right?" She cocked an eyebrow, knowingly playing the guilt card.

I laughed, but she was right.

"Thanks," I said, pulling her into another quick hug. "Really. I needed this."

"Anytime, hon. Shoot me a text if you want to get together this week, okay? I'm going upstate over the weekend but any other time…"

I nodded and watched as she circled around to the driver's side.

When I took a deep breath, all of my stress went with it on the exhale.

All the secrets I'd been holding onto, all the worries.

I felt lighter now that it was out there. Maybe now it would be easier to tell him that I was job searching. And perhaps I'd take Kate's advice and consider hanging around Cold Springs a while longer.

Skyside towered overhead and I had to squint into the sunlight to see the very top. Somewhere up there was the little bedroom I'd grown used to. Watched by Max's figurines on those shelves; I still got a chuckle out of them waking up each morning.

My phone vibrated and I stepped to the side of the main doors.

You heading back soon? Max's text. It sent a hopeful thrill through me thanks to my conversation with Kate. Did he miss me? Did he want to veg out, watch a movie together with Rosie curled up between us?

On my way now, I replied.

The doorman, who had grown used to me, gave me a polite if not somewhat vacant smile. I ignored the two women at the front desk, recognizing the rude one from my first day here, and headed to the quiet hallway with the penthouse elevator.

The button lit up almost immediately, which was surprising.

My phone chimed again. This time with an email alert. A quick glance at the notification told me that one of the jobs I'd applied to last week was trying to set up an interview with me. Stomach churning with nerves and guilt, I didn't look as the elevator doors opened up, and I walked right in.

Immediately crashing into someone.

Someone who could only be Max, given their height and the way they caught me quickly around the waist.

"Woah," he laughed, steadying me but not letting go, "where's the fire?"

I gaped up at him, caught off guard by how close we were. Our hips and stomachs were pressed together. He had taken a wide stance to brace himself when he caught me and my legs were between his, growing weaker by the second as I took him in.

He wore basketball shorts that hung low on his waist and a dri-fit shirt, that outlined his chiseled chest. My mouth watered and I barely noticed his quick glance upwards as the elevator doors shut.

"Oh—" I rushed out, righting myself and stepping back. I didn't get too far; the elevator was a decent size, but suddenly seemed hot and tight with the two of us in it. Nervously, I reached up and checked my ponytail, then straightened my shirt.

"Sorry, you're heading out?"

"Just for a quick run." His lopsided grin and narrow eyes told me he had an idea of where my mind had gone only moments ago. I clamped my mouth shut, trying to think of a retort.

It's been a while since I'd been with anyone. I'm definitely not affected by your bare skin pressed up against me. Not at all. Or the way those shorts are hanging low. Or the sliver of stomach visible when you—

I shook myself, blinking back to reality and feeling a blush set in. Max's grin only widened.

"I'll take the ride up with you. I actually forgot my hat." he said. "Monica's upstairs with the girls. I didn't want to rush your lunch with Kate."

With a nod, I tried to look away, at anything else. There weren't many options in the elevator and we were only at the 28th floor. He leaned against the wall, his shirt riding up again to expose that tan piece of flesh that made my thighs quiver.

What was wrong with me? One lunch with Kate where I confessed my attraction to Max and I was suddenly falling apart?

Or maybe it was the near kiss from the other night.

We made some small talk about our day and finally, the doors opened. We both stepped into the foyer and he opened the door for me, his hand ghosting the small of my back as he called out, "Rosie, Adrianna! Lacey is here. Monica, thanks again—I'll see you next week."

Monica, the housekeeper and sometimes sitter, called out a thanks from somewhere within the apartment. He smiled at me as I stepped inside.

"I'll see you later?" he asked, taking a few lazy steps backwards, that silly grin on his face.

"Yeah," I replied, still lost in a haze of trying not to imagine how fit he'd look jogging down the street. "Yeah, I'll have dinner ready by the time you're done. Enjoy your run!"

Shutting the door behind me, I let out a deep breath and deflated.

This man was going to be the death of me. Hopefully, that email about a job would prove to be fruitful. Even if the thought of leaving the penthouse, and Rosie and Max, killed me a little bit.

Just then, Rosie and her friend, Adrianna, came running in and began babbling about a new kid at school who just started today. I chatted along with them, moving into the kitchen to start dinner.

Chapter 11

Max

It was an absolutely perfect day out for some one-on-one time with Rosie. I couldn't have asked for better. The sun was bright and the temp was mild. A t-shirt and jeans felt comfortable. Rosie flitted about the park in a dress and striped tights, quickly making new friends and greeting old ones with no hesitation.

Sometimes, usually late at night when I was going through a list of regrets, I wished I'd had another kid. Not sure how it would've worked since Skylar and I barely managed to make it past Rosie's infancy, but it would have been nice for her to grow up with a sibling. Watching her with other kids made my heart ache, and made me proud all at once. She was just the best.

"Dad," she said breathlessly, skidding to a stop on the sandy mat in front of me. "Stewart's mom wants to know if I can go to his birthday party next weekend. Can I? Please? Please, please?"

I looked up and met Nicole Santigado's eyes; her son Stewart was shy and was one of the kids Rosie was most attached to despite the vast differences in their personalities.

"Sure," I said, giving Nicole a polite nod. She waved back happily, interpreting that I was agreeing. "Ask Stewart what time we should be there."

I gave her a gentle nudge toward the jungle gym and watched as she fearlessly climbed a miniature rock wall with knotted ropes spilling down it. Stewart waited at the top, near a slide, the shy blonde boy pushing his chunky glasses up his nose.

My mind went to Lacey and her glasses. How she'd whipped out a pair I'd never seen before the other day. Cat eyes, or something like that; curved lenses that gave her a wicked look, backed up by the devilish grin she'd given Rosie during a tickle fight.

Another twenty minutes went by and I basked in the ability to finally relax a little. Steven had insisted that I take the weekend off, putting Victor in charge of any incidents that cropped up. At first, Victor had seemed confident, but it was easy to see through. Actually having to step up and take responsibility, while also potentially dealing with the fallout of whatever decisions he made, made Victor nervous. It was why he'd never get too far on his own. He wasn't willing to take a leap.

Following that train of thought, my mind flashed back to a hurried conversation I'd had with Steven in the main lobby at Journey Studios.

"So you asked Lacey out?"

I looked at him in surprise. "No? Where did you hear that?"

"Kate said they went dress shopping a few days ago for a date night. You sure you didn't finally take the leap?"

When the expression on my face changed from confused to irritation, he'd groaned and given me a nudge.

"I'm telling you. You better be careful. If you don't snatch her up…"

Somebody else will.

With a heavy sigh, I stood from the bench and called Rosie. She pouted but came down the slide anyway. Waving goodbye over her shoulder, she stumbled into me and slipped her little hand in mine.

We started the walk to Skyside, along a route where there just happened to be an ice cream parlor.

"Maybe you and Lacey can get Stewart a gift sometime this week," I mused aloud, swinging our arms as we walked. "After school, or before the party this weekend."

Rosie nodded absently, her little eyes scanning the busy streets. She was inquisitive and I loved that about her, but it also scared me a bit. What did she get up to when I wasn't around? What *would* she get up to when I wasn't around, as she got older?

"Will Lacey be here for my birthday?" Rosie asked abruptly, looking up at me.

I blanked, not knowing the answer. Rosie's birthday was months away, in August. When Lacey and I had set this whole arrangement up I'd told her I'd only need help for two months, tops.

But if I was being honest, I hadn't started looking for another nanny. I knew I had to—Lacey couldn't stay with us forever. Definitely not in the penthouse, and I wasn't sure how she felt about the city long-term.

Either way, I had to bite the bullet and at least get a job posting up. No matter how heavy my heart was at the thought.

"I'm not sure," I answered my daughter evasively. "We'll have to see. If she's not still living here though, I'm sure she'd come back for your birthday."

Rosie's shoulders drooped and she scuffed her shoes on the sidewalk. I looked up ahead, at the rainbow-colored façade of the ice cream parlor, and prayed it would lighten her mood a little bit.

"I didn't realize you liked her so much," I said honestly, holding the door open. Rosie stepped inside, but instead of running to the freezer chest and looking over the colorful offerings, she kept close by.

"Lacey's fun," she said matter-of-factly, as if I should know that. I tried to suppress a grin. "She makes really good snacks and she helps me with my homework sometimes. And she likes to go out to the park. Or on a walk."

Ah—as much as we'd loved Ann, she hadn't been big on the outdoors. A true city girl, she lived for being inside, no matter what the weather was doing. Rosie really enjoyed spending lots of time outside, as most kids do, and Ann wasn't up for it.

Despite having grown up in Cold Springs, somehow Rosie got the outdoor bug that Lacey and I'd had growing up. We'd spent every summer riding our bikes around our small hometown or swimming. In the winter, we built forts and went sledding.

None of that could really happen here, of course, for Rosie. But someday maybe…

"I think we should ask her when we get home," Rosie said determinedly, eyeing the sprinkles on top of the case as I ordered us two waffle cones.

"We'll see what she's up to, hun. We don't want to interrupt her if she's working."

Rosie's nose scrunched up. "Working? I thought her work was to watch me?"

Giving her hand a little tug to get her full attention, I explained: "Watching you isn't Lacey's job. She's helping us out right now, but we're going to find you another nanny. And when we do, she'll go back to her own work."

My little girl looked crestfallen, but asked, "At the library?"

I nodded. "Probably, yeah. Maybe when you're out of school this summer we can make a trip and go visit her."

That perked her up a bit, but I couldn't get rid of the heavy feeling in my gut at the thought of Lacey not being around. Which was crazy—she'd only been here for a few weeks, and already I was so attached.

How had we separated so easily when we were younger?

Ah, of course. Craig.

There had been a slow year of Lacey disappearing little by little, her time entirely consumed by Craig.

Good riddance. I'd always thought he was a jerk, very full of himself.

The cashier handed us our ice cream with a smile and Rosie practically dragged me out into the sunshine. She wanted to sit on a nearby bench, afraid that the sprinkles would fall off if we kept walking, and I gave in, wanting to enjoy the day.

My phone buzzed once and I ignored it.

Probably Steven, checking in to see if I wanted to grab a drink.

But then it buzzed again, twice in quick succession. And then a third time.

I froze, grip tightening on the waffle cone enough that it cracked slightly. Then the ringing started.

With a sigh, I tried to ignore the downcast look Rosie gave me as I picked up the call.

"Hello?"

"Mr. Munroe," a harried voice said on the other line, "I'm sorry to bother you, but you might want to come into the office."

"I'm sorry, but this is my weekend off," I replied firmly, trying to place the voice. It was familiar. But we had limited staff on the weekends. Basically just maintenance to fix any issues that popped up while everyone else was away.

"I know Mr. Munroe, but Mr. Bolton asked me to call you—"

Victor. Victor actually had the guts to call me on my day off.

Why was I not surprised?

I ground my jaw, letting the silence settle across the line. I wanted it understood how unhappy I was about this. I wanted Victor shaking in his shoes at least a little bit.

"If it's not an emergency—"

"It kind of is," the unidentified voice broke in quickly. "I'm sorry, Mr. Munroe, but it's about the Underground."

My blood went cold. Rosie watched the hand holding the ice cream cone slowly drop into my lap, and I knew without having to see her expression that she understood what that meant.

It was nice while it lasted.

"I can't come in immediately," I said gruffly, "but I'll be there within the hour. Tell Victor to begin drafting a memo to the heads of each division. We need to nip this in the bud."

I waited for verbal confirmation, then hung up.

The Underground was one of the most popular video game review platforms out there, frequented by hundreds of thousands of gamers a day. If there was an emergency centered around the Underground, it could only mean that there was another leak out there.

This time, front and center.

Please let it be old material, I begged as I gathered up our things and swiftly shepherded Rosie down the street. Her eyes were downcast, the ice cream forgotten and dripping down her knuckles.

But I knew that if it was coming from the Underground, whatever they had was earth-shattering. This platform didn't play fair and employed a huge legal team. If there was one thing myself and my competitors in the industry agreed on, it was that someone had to take down the Underground.

A few blocks away from Skyside, I looked up and saw the familiar glint of our apartment thirty-eight floors up. It was just past noon and then sun rode high in the sky, warming the air between the buildings to a comfortable temperature.

If I wasn't going in, how would the rest of the day play out?

Chasing Rosie around the apartment? Listening to her chatter away as I worked on personal projects? Catching up with Lacey and finally getting to ask her more about the last few years of her life, the specifics?

Lacey.

Fumbling my phone out of my pocket, I found her name quickly and hit call. She picked up on the second ring.

"Everything okay?" she asked, as if clairvoyant.

"No, actually. There's an emergency and I need you."

The words spilled out quickly. I didn't think twice about how they sounded. I didn't care, it was true. I needed her.

"Of course, Max," Lace answered immediately, her voice steady and reassuring. "Whatever you need. I'm here."

The anxious bubble in my chest burst at those words, and my grip on Rosie's hand loosened.

For once, it didn't feel like the world was ending, due to a panicked phone call or text from work.

I still wasn't thrilled about having to go in on my weekend off, but this just made me more resolute: as soon as *Apocalypse Summit* was released and out there in the world, I was going to step back.

As we marched toward home, I realized that there were more important things waiting for me.

Chapter 12

Max

On Tuesday things calmed down enough for me to finally circle back to that promise I'd made Lacey.

Dinner. A night out, just the two of us. I've been looking forward to it.

It had been a hectic few days with the Underground leaking some major footage from *Apocalypse*, but the PR and legal team had come together to denounce the platform's actions and we were garnering support not only from competitors, but gamers.

Seemed like everyone wanted to enjoy *Apocalypse* with fresh eyes.

Luckily the frames they'd gotten their hands on didn't reveal anything major about the game. Still, I'd spent hours in my office, and later at home in bed, wracking my brain.

Who was selling us out? Who was leaking the game?

The entire IT team was tracking a crooked trail, but hadn't found anything definitive. We'd narrowed down the possibilities to about thirty people or so who touched the designs in the form they'd appeared, but all we could do was wait.

Hopefully the rumor mill would start up and point us in the right direction.

Gerald and I stood down on the street in front of Skyside, waiting for Lacey. She'd been finishing up a book with Rosie before Gianna, the sitter for tonight, took over. I was grateful to see Rosie so attached to Lacey, but if they didn't hurry things up we'd be late for our reservation.

"Special night, Mr. Munroe?" Gerald asked, shifting his small frame from one foot to another. I smiled, gazing around at the lamp-lit streets.

"You could say that, Gerald. I haven't had any one-on-one time with Lacey yet. It'll be good to catch up."

Gerald nodded knowingly, his face somber. "The missus and I used to make time once a month. We'd go the whole nine yards; dress up, get a reservation, I'd buy her favorite flowers. It was what kept our love alive."

I gave him a nervous smile, tempted to explain that Lacey and I weren't exactly a couple. But before I could open my mouth, the doors opened and she slipped out.

She wore a navy dress that swirled around her calves and hugged her upper body tightly. It was sleeveless, a halter that showed off her collarbones, and Gerald and I both stared—one in surprise, the other in appreciation.

Okay...both of us in appreciation.

"You look wonderful, Miss Weaver." Gerald spoke first, making me flush and bite back a stutter.

Lacey gave him a small smile as she came up to my side.

"Thank you, Gerald. Please, call me Lacey, I insist."

Gerald lifted a brow at me, and I hurried to open the back door, as she carefully climbed inside.

"Where to, sir?" Gerald asked.

I gave him the name of one of the best restaurants in town. Lacey had insisted more than once that we didn't need to go anywhere fancy, and I'd been tempted to just bring her to a food truck...but couldn't resist.

Gerald nodded approvingly and she shot me a curious look, but I only smiled.

The back seat of the Rover suddenly felt much smaller than it ever had before. The space between Lacey and I was practically non-existent as our thighs touched, then shifted apart. In the rearview mirror I caught sight of Gerald's knowing smile and felt my stomach twist with nerves.

Of course, I had nothing to worry about; this was *Lacey*.

My friend. My confidant. She'd seen me at my worst, covered in acne, resigned to in-school suspension after getting caught gaming in class, those weeks after my dad's death.

But I couldn't stop staring at the woman standing next to me.

I'd missed her smile and laughter most of all. It was good to have her back, but my heart also ached at all the lost time.

"This place is fabulous," she murmured, glancing around appreciatively. This was one of the few upscale restaurants I enjoyed, mostly because there was still a level of privacy and respect. It wasn't uncommon to see actors, musicians, or politicians there, but everyone left each other alone. The waitstaff was polite and never asked for photos. You could come here and relax and have a quiet meal.

Which was what I wanted. What I realized, sitting across from Lacey, I'd been missing for a long time.

"I wanted to properly thank you," I said, pulling her chair out as we arrived at our table, "I really owe you one, Lace. For saving me. And Rosie."

She smiled at the mention of my daughter. She'd admitted earlier that Rosie had helped her decide how to wear her hair. She had left it wavy and tumbling down her back.

For the hundredth time since she arrived I found myself having to hold back. It took everything in me not to stand up, lean across the table and kiss her.

And the best part was no one here would care. It wouldn't be reported to the news outlets.

But it didn't feel quite right, and as Lacey took another fleeting look around the dimly lit room, I knew it was because this wasn't really us.

"Sorry," I said with an awkward smile. "We should've just gotten take-out."

She giggled, picking at the risotto in front of her and having a sip of wine. "No, this is nice. I'm sorry. I'm a little uncomfortable."

"What is there to be uncomfortable about?"

Lacey's eyes ran quickly over my chest and then she blushed.

I cocked an eyebrow. Pushed my plate away and leaned in.

Perhaps the wine was getting me to a little...

"Remember that time the four of us went skinny dipping in the neighbor's pool and we all got caught red handed and had to get out of the pool naked? I've never put on my clothes faster in my whole life..."

She laughed wholeheartedly, a belly laugh that made my grin widen. The blush still stained her cheeks. "I remember it well," she said, "who could forget your skinny little butt running for your clothes."

Puffing my cheeks out, I pretended to look offended. "Really? Do you have any idea how many people want to get a look at what I'm hiding under this?" I gestured grandly at the basic suit and tie get-up.

Now there was a mischievous twinkle in her eye as she leaned in, too. "Who's to say I won't double cross you?" she practically purred, sending a shiver down my spine and heat to my groin. "I could probably make a pretty penny off a few surreptitious photos." The wine was definitely emboldening Lacey as well.

My mind should've been triggered into thinking of the *Apocalypse* leak, but instead I was too focused on coming up with what kind of scenarios could get me into that kind of trouble. If we went back to the apartment and she told me to lay it all out, holding onto a Polaroid, it would be hard to say no.

"I think I could come up with a way to distract you from your wicked intentions."

For a brief moment I realized how much closer we were, leaning in. Lacey's arms were crossed and the halter dress lifted her breasts deliciously close to the square-cut neckline. My eyes darted down as my legs widened, trying to make room for the slowly growing problem I was now dealing with...

Good thing we still had dessert to get through before I had to get up from the table.

I opened my mouth—not sure what I intended on saying—but was interrupted by an excited female voice.

"Max! I wasn't expecting to see you here, it's been months!"

Lacey's gaze went to the spot over my left shoulder, and I turned.

Andrea Gutierrez, a therapist that Rosie saw for two years after Skylar and I ended things, was passing by with her wife, a well-known news anchor. Their entire relationship and marriage was kept very private. Something I was envious of.

"Andrea, hi! It's great to see you both."

"You as well. I've been keeping up with Journey Studios so I know how busy you've been. I hope Rosie is doing well?"

Out of the corner of my eye I saw Lacey's expression go blank as she watched us chat. Her shoulders slowly slumped and she put her chin in her hand.

"This is Lacey, my—"

"Nanny," Lacey interrupted with a tight smile.

Andrea raised her eyebrows. Her wife gave her a small nudge and signaled that she'd be waiting outside.

"And an old friend," I said, giving Lacey a questioning look. She looked embarrassed for a moment. Andrea held a manicured hand out.

"It's nice to meet you. I love your dress."

"Thanks," she replied awkwardly. "I love yours, too."

Unsurprisingly, Andrea looked stunning in a fitted white off-the-shoulder dress. Her close-cropped hair looked like something out of a black and white movie, seductive and flawless. She gave Lacey a warm smile.

"I'm sorry for interrupting your evening, it's not every day you run into Max Munroe. I'll let you two be. It was nice to see you. Tell Rosie I said hello and I hope she's doing well."

And with that, Andrea waltzed off toward the exit.

A blanket of confusion settled over me as I turned to Lacey.

Chapter 13

Lacey

The short ride back to Skyside was awkward. Awkward enough that Gerald repeatedly caught my eye in the rearview mirror and looked away hurriedly.

I ran over the last few minutes of dinner in my head, feeling like a complete idiot.

The woman, Andrea, hadn't been anything other than nice. So why was I so defensive?

Again I went through the play-by-play; the way her hand had settled comfortably on Max's shoulder as she walked by. Her gorgeous figure, not to mention that of the *other* woman she was with. The pair were flawless and at the moment I'd known that I could never compete with either of them.

Andrea in particular had given off an air of sophistication and confidence that shook me out of the flirty mood Max and I had created.

It was like crashing back to reality.

"Have a good night, Mr. Munroe, Miss Lacey."

I gave Gerald a small smile as I slipped across the seat, hesitating before taking Max's hand to help me out. An electric tingle went through my fingers when they met his and I pulled them back quickly.

The look on Max's face, I knew, meant he was a little offended and trying to play it off. We walked side by side into the quiet lobby and to the elevator, where we stood in uncomfortable silence.

"I'm sorry," he finally said, sounding baffled as he stared at the metal doors in front of us. "I know now that wasn't really the dinner you wanted. I shouldn't have made you go."

Shame rushed through me and I almost reached out to touch his arm, but stopped myself.

"No," I responded, shaking my head, "it was wonderful. Really. The restaurant was beautiful and the food was great. I'm sorry…"

I trailed off, not knowing what to say.

I'm sorry I acted like a sulky brat for no reason? I'm sorry I embarrassed you in front of your friend?

I scrunched up my face as it sank in just how annoyed with myself I was. He had only been trying to do something nice, and instead I'd ruined the whole night.

The elevator arrived and he held out an arm, gesturing for me to step in first. I did, looking down at my shoes and smoothing my dress once the doors shut again.

What had I planned on happening, though? Kate's fairytale story of Max sweeping me off my feet and the two of us admitting how mad we were about each other? That didn't happen in real life. Especially when the feelings were one-sided.

It seemed to take forever to reach the penthouse, and when we did he opened the door without a word and greeted the babysitter. I slipped by them, taking off my heels and retreating to the living room where I'd left a book and my laptop earlier.

Better to start my job search back up sooner rather than later. At the rate I was going, it wouldn't take too long for me to die of embarrassment.

Just as I'd hefted everything into my arms, he appeared at my side. He looked tired and let down and I felt horrible about it.

"I'm sorry—" I blurted out again.

The only light in the apartment came from the full moon outside and the dim blue light that the city always seemed to generate. It softened the edges, and as I took him in he looked a little more like his old self. Hands shoved in his pockets, suit jacket undone, hair mussed up. He had a shadow of stubble. I wanted to reach up and run my thumb over it but suppressed the urge.

"I wasn't expecting to see Andrea there," he said right as I'd stepped past him to head to my room.

I stopped, half-turning and pretending to be surprised. Even though all I'd been thinking about was the woman and how faultless she was.

"Oh, it's fine," I said, voice unnaturally light even to my ears, "it's a big city but I'm sure you still run into exes all the time."

He frowned and I whipped around quickly, making for the hallway. But he caught my elbow.

"Ex? Andrea isn't an ex."

The grip on my laptop and book tightened as I finally looked into his eyes. "She seemed pretty familiar with Rosie."

I couldn't imagine that Max let just anyone get to know his daughter. Rosie hadn't mentioned an Andrea before, but then I'd never asked her about the women her dad possibly dated. It would be inappropriate.

Slowly, the corner of his mouth lifted in a smile.

"Andrea was her therapist. She's a child psychologist. Rosie saw her after the separation."

My eyes widened in realization. But a part of me still found it hard to believe that Max and Andrea hadn't had something going on. The woman was gorgeous and seemed so excited to see him.

"She, uh, regressed," he explained, struggling to look for the right words. "Went back to sucking her thumb when Skylar moved out. And she started to throw tantrums. I had a friend who recommended Andrea."

"Oh," I said numbly. At the same time, a weight was lifting off my chest.

"And if I had to guess, they were probably out celebrating her wife's promotion to head anchor—"

Oh, no.

Oh, I was an idiot. A complete and total idiot.

With a groan, I dropped my head back. "The other woman. Her wife. Of course. I'm so sorry. I didn't mean to embarrass you."

But he was laughing, a low rumble that made my stomach flip as he stepped closer. I wasn't sure what he was doing until he took the laptop and book from me, moving away to place them on the living room table.

"You know," he said, coming back to stand right in front of me, his voice still low. In the dark, his eyes flashed that caramel color. Like liquid. "I never took you for the jealous sort."

A blush set my face on fire as I looked down at my feet again. "I—I just felt out of place," I tried to explain, stumbling over the words. "You have such a lavish lifestyle. Really, Max, the restaurant was wonderful, and not one I could ever afford to go to so thank you for the treat." I was rambling, but couldn't stop myself as he inched closer. "I know you keep saying I'm doing you and Rosie a favor but I'm not really cut out for this life—"

He gripped my elbows, tugging me closer so that I could feel the heat coming off his body. My breath caught.

"You're *too* good for this life, Lacey," he murmured.

And then he leaned in and kissed me.

The next day I was so caught up in daydreaming about the kiss that I didn't hear the knocking at the front door until Rosie popped into my room.

"Are you going to get that?" she asked with the excitement of a little kid, "Or can I?"

"I'll get it," I answered, pushing away the memory of Max's lips crushed against mine in the dark of the apartment. All my senses had lit up feeling the press of his hand on my lower back, guiding me closer, the taste of wine as his tongue swiped my lower lip...

Rosie skidded by the room again, on the way to her own. "They're still knocking!"

I hurried out to the foyer and pressed the button for the small camera just outside of the elevator.

Long, tan legs, trendy silver booties and a skin-tight dress.

Opening the door, I stood face to face with Skylar West. As if she'd been summoned by the devil himself.

She looked me over critically. I wore sweatpants and an oversized t-shirt, my glasses askew.

"I'm here for Rosie," she said icily.

It all came rushing back. A few days ago Max had mentioned that Skylar would be by to bring Rosie to the premiere of a superhero movie she really wanted to see. They were picking up two of her school friends on the way.

"Mom!" Rosie called, skidding out into the living room somewhere behind me. Skylar's eyes softened as she looked at her daughter. "I forgot this was the day! I need to pick out an outfit! Can you wait?"

The ghost of a smile on Skylar's lips dropped my guard and I stepped back. She sent me a glance before walking in as if she owned the place, slinging her bag on the bench by the door. She moved down the hallway as if it was a runway and disappeared into the apartment.

I'm not sure why she knocked this time since last time she chose to waltz right on in. I wondered if he asked that she knock since I was living here now.

With a sigh, I followed. But I knew Rosie was excited for her big day out and it was oddly comforting to know that Skylar was willing to make her daughter a priority, even if she wasn't here 24/7. As much as it stung to admit it, Max was lucky.

His ex wanted to live her life, sure. But she was there for Rosie when it mattered and made sure to leave her with memorable time spent together.

As Skylar sashayed through the living room with me close behind, my muscles clenched in anticipation.

Would she be able to tell? Just the night before Max and I stood right *there*, glued together and out of breath.

The kiss had gotten out of hand quickly and a small part of my brain focused on the fact that I was probably coming off as desperate, practically climbing into his arms. But if I was desperate, so was he. I felt his quick inhale when he pulled back to check if I was okay with the situation. Pressing forward on the balls of my feet was all the sign he needed. He dove right back in, devouring my mouth in a searing kiss and lightly licking my bottom lip.

The kiss sent a thrill of fire up my spine and to my core.

How many stolen moments had I dreamed of kissing Max Munroe? Sure, most of those daydreams took place when we were teenagers, with raging hormones running through our veins.

But it hadn't felt all that different last night. I'd still ached for him, almost going limp in his arms as he stepped into my space and firmly placed his hand across my lower back.

Skylar threw a glance over her shoulder and I stumbled, flushing.

She couldn't see it on my face, could she? Oh, God. This was a nightmare. Stuck in the apartment of the man I've been pining for with his ex-wife. Not to mention, after a night where I'd made a complete ass of myself.

Skylar turned the corner and, unexpectedly, stopped. I skidded into her. Somehow she managed to stay perfectly balanced in those booties with the wedged heels. She looked disgusted as she steadied me.

"So. You've made yourself at home."

The last time she'd been here to get Rosie, the door to my room was shut. And she hadn't stayed long once they returned from their day out.

But now the bedroom door stood open, the comforter slightly rumbled and a big pillow halfway down the bed. My laptop was propped open on top of it.

Too late, I realized what was on the screen.

Skylar's eyes narrowed.

For a moment the only sound in the apartment was from Rosie's room as she dug through the closet. Then Skylar's light-colored eyes met mine and the irritation melted from her face. She looked tired and... sad?

"He's having a hard time with that, isn't he?"

She was referring to the article up on the Underground's website. I'd read it that morning, curious how bad it really was. He was more stressed than ever. Now that I thought about it, dinner last night had been the first time he'd relaxed a little in the last few weeks.

"Yeah, he is," I confirmed, voice quiet so as not to alert Rosie that anything was wrong. Not that she hadn't picked up on her dad's anxiety.

Skylar took a deep breath. "Max always hated the unsavoriness of the gaming industry. He just wanted to create." A thin, somehow pretty line formed between her brows. "It's this kind of thing that makes him regret ever starting Journey."

I bit my lip, but couldn't keep the words in now that there was a sliver of camaraderie between us.

"I don't know. He never could've kept his ideas to himself. It was bound to happen, but... you're right. Things like this break him down."

Skylar nodded, her eyes far away as she turned away from the bedroom and moved slowly toward Rosie's. The tension left my body as I followed, wondering what was going through her mind.

Rosie chattered away when Skylar appeared in the doorway, asking her mom which pair of pants she should wear and then agonizing over what shoes went with the outfit. Like mother, like daughter; but Skylar kept her cool and let Rosie make the ultimate decision.

Then the two of them were striding toward the front door, Rosie out of breath with excitement and telling Skylar, "Hurry! Jo and Kristen are waiting!"

Skylar and I wore twin indulgent smiles as we stood in the doorway.

I wasn't quite sure what to say, but settled on, "Have fun, you two," giving Rosie a small wave as they waited for the elevator to arrive.

Skylar gave me one last appraising look, then stepped into the elevator and disappeared behind the doors.

Chapter 14

Max

For two days I'd been on edge, my body coiled and waiting for release. Partly due to stress, and partly due to lust.

It was hard to be around Lacey without thinking of the kiss. Not that we'd spent much time around each other since we kissed.

No, work was keeping me busy. IT notified me the morning after the dinner that they'd narrowed the list of suspects down to twenty. A number that eased some of the pressure, but only had me restless in a different way.

Did I really want to know who it was? I pictured the moment over and over, a faceless employee in my office, waiting to be reprimanded and then fired. The feeling of betrayal...

Whoever this was, their career would be ruined after this. They'd never be able to find a job in the industry again once they were exposed, and it was my duty to be transparent. Even to my competitors. No one deserved to have their work leaked like this.

"You ready?" Aisha asked, popping into my office.

I blinked at her in surprise, then looked at the clock. An hour had flown by.

"Yeah. Yeah, sure."

She gave me a critical once-over.

"You're not wearing the jacket I got you."

Ugh. The faux-leather monstrosity that creaked every time I moved.

"I think this is more my style," I replied, trying to sound confident as I smoothed down the light blue button-down. She's lucky I didn't have a t-shirt on.

She squinted at me, but gave in.

Aisha had an interesting background. She was in her early forties and, decades ago, had been in school for design. Specifically, fashion design. It was part of what had captured my interest during her interview; having another creative mind on the team, not just a business person who wanted to play the media and industry's games.

Finally, she gave a decisive nod and disappeared.

"Let's go, then."

Within minutes we were taking an inconspicuous car to *Miley & Dodd*, the morning show Aisha had lined up an interview with. They aired every day until 11:45 am and were surprisingly popular among the younger generations, talking to a wide variety of experts and interesting people.

Aisha insisted that I was interesting, but I disagreed.

"Either way," she'd waved it off, "they sought us out, which means there's a lot of anticipation around *Apocalypse Summit*. You should be happy."

I should be, but I wasn't. I hated doing interviews. While *Miley & Dodd* were known for diversity, they were also known for verbal left-hooks that often left their interviewees speechless. For some unfortunate few, they ended up divulging some things they wanted to keep private, completely caught off guard.

For the entire twenty-minute ride to the studio my shoulders were tight with anticipation. What would they dig into? The Underground's article would come up, undoubtedly. Then what? Skylar being in town?

"Here," Aisha said, as if reading my mind. She handed me two pages stapled together. "These are the questions we agreed upon. Nothing too crazy, all standard, maybe you can throw in a little more detail now that we're nearing release."

"And now that some of those details are already out there," I muttered, but she ignored me.

At the rear of the building we were ushered inside and Aisha handed me over to a small team of people who moved and shifted endlessly, like an undulating mass of arms. They corralled me into a room, applied a light coat of makeup—which made me think of Lacey, and smile impulsively—would she still want to kiss me if I had lip balm on?

Within ten minutes Aisha was back.

"Ready?"

I nodded, taking a deep breath and trying to ignore the jitters that still overtook me at every interview. Didn't matter that I'd been doing this for a decade, that Aisha had gotten me public speaking lessons years ago, that I knew all the tricks of the trade. Bite an apple if your mouth is dry, suck a lemon if you're salivating from nerves.

Every. Single. Time. I felt sick to my stomach and hated it.

Better to just get it over with.

Behind the navy curtain, I listened as Miley Lewis led into my introduction. Then Dodd Roberts enthusiastically announced that I was here, and I stepped out onto the small stage with a locked-on grin.

Handshakes all around, that uncomfortable high chair that left my feet dangling. Conscious of Aisha gesturing out of the corner of my eye, I hooked my heels onto the bottom rung and tried to look confident.

"We're here today with Max Munroe of Journey Studios to talk about his upcoming game, *Apocalypse Summit*. Much anticipated according to the critics out there—Max, are you expecting a big turnout for the release?"

Already my cheeks were aching from keeping the smile glued on.

"Yes, Dodd, we are. We've already sold out of preorder slots and we're in negotiations to move up to the next major phase of production. I want to get this game out to our fans as soon as possible so they aren't left waiting."

Miley, who sat to my left, leaned in and placed a hand on my thigh. It was a flirty move, but I deadened my eyes intentionally and felt her cool off toward me.

"Max, the world is still surprised that you're single years after the split with Skylar West."

I interrupted before she had the chance to fully drag the conversation to my personal life. "Well, I always want to produce quality content for our fans, so I spend my time at the office these days instead of dating. Journey's team of almost two hundred employees is incredibly dedicated, but it wouldn't be a far reach to say I practically live at the office."

Scattered laughter out in the audience widened my smile as I gazed out. With the lights, it was impossible to see who was out there, but that was probably for the better. I could already feel my armpits sweating.

On my other side, Dodd chuckled.

"Ah, he's an evasive one Miley! You'll have to try harder than that. What can you tell us about *Apocalypse Summit*? Word on the street is we may have already gotten an unofficial reveal thanks to an overzealous individual."

My smile tightened and I tried for a sympathetic but firm response. "That's true, unfortunately. We're doing what we can to find out where the leak came from, and whoever had a hand in it will be held accountable. That being said, *Apocalypse Summit* has more than a few surprises in store for our fans. The taste you got with the leaked footage is nothing compared to what awaits you, so keep that in mind."

Dodd seemed satisfied to move onto the next question, but instead Miley cut in once more.

"We've *also* heard rumors of Skylar West hanging around town, and we can't help but wonder… are there still sparks between the two of you?"

I managed to suppress my sigh at the inevitable question, knowing that somewhere Aisha was turning red and ready to fight. She took agreed-upon questions very seriously and, somehow, still hadn't learned that they'd change the rules whenever they could.

It was all a part of the game.

"Skylar and I co-parent our daughter together, but no, we are not in a romantic relationship. I'm sure she'd be very supportive of my statement that we care for and want the best for one another, but we're happier as friends and co-parents."

Miley sat back, put out with the response.

"Is there anyone special in your life? A guy like you… it's surprising no one has snatched you up!"

The look in her eye had me questioning whether she was asking for the audience or for herself. In the spirit of playing along, I decided to lob her an easy tidbit.

"Actually, there is someone special, but for now we've decided to keep our relationship private."

On the sidelines, Aisha's brows rose. I could feel her waiting as the interview went on for another fifteen minutes or so, Dodd asking questions about the industry and upcoming creations while Miley continued to pry inappropriately. But this wasn't my first time around the block, and I shut her down easily.

When the cameras finally cut off for a commercial break and their next segment, I slid out of the chair immediately without giving Miley a second glance.

"What was that?" Aisha asked as she turned and followed me down the hallway, back to the small room where my bag was. I waved off the staff who were offering to wash the makeup off.

"What was what?" I asked, knowing exactly what she meant but feeling exhausted already. And it wasn't even noon.

"Just tell me this," she asked briskly, giving the ajar door a glance, "was that the truth, or a lie to draw attention? You know I don't care about who you're dating, but it would help to know what's real and what's not."

I gave her a quick grin as we headed out the door and into the waiting sedan. I'd only have to be at Journey for a few more hours, and then I could get home and relax for the rest of the day. It was much needed at this point.

"It's not exactly the truth," I said, catching the annoyed roll of Aisha's eyes. "I'm not trying to be evasive. There's someone special, we're not... it's not official or anything like that. I'm not even sure if she feels the same way."

A laugh bubbled from Aisha abruptly. "So you have *intentions* with this person, but you don't know if she likes you?"

"Yes," I confirmed, feeling my neck heat and rubbing at it.

"That's very high school of you," Aisha deadpanned, but she gave me a reassuring smile. "Just let me know if it turns into anything 'official' so I can field the media, alright?"

I hadn't had to admit it out loud yet, but Steven was right—my high school crush on Lacey had never dissipated. In fact, these days it seemed to be stronger, if that kiss was any indication.

My body was practically throbbing at all hours wanting to be close to her. And the crazy thing was it wasn't just sexual. Not really. I couldn't wrap my mind around the possibility that she might let me touch her that way and bring her pleasure. It was enough that she'd let me kiss her.

As we pulled into the lot at Journey, I got lost in that heart-stopping moment again. Instinct taking over, pulling her closer and pressing my lips to hers. Waiting with baited breath for her to push me away.

Instead, she'd melted into me. Just eagerly enough that I went back in and deepened the kiss.

In the dark my fingers trailed down her spine and I instinctively pressed my knee between hers, pulling her closer.

For a few blissful minutes I lost myself in the fantasy I'd been drowning in for years: what it would be like to kiss Lacey Weaver.

Now I knew, but the problem was… it wasn't enough.

I wanted more. I ached for her. And if I was being honest with myself, when I'd answered Miley Lewis I wasn't lying. There was someone; I wanted her. I wanted her to want me too.

Now I needed to man up and tell her the truth. I needed to make her mine.

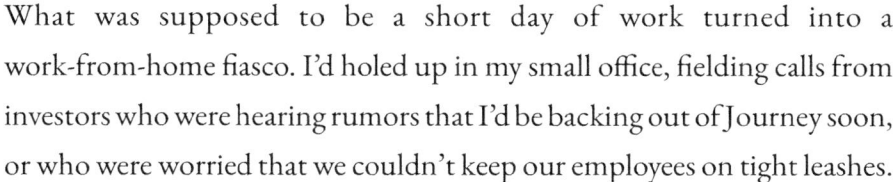

What was supposed to be a short day of work turned into a work-from-home fiasco. I'd holed up in my small office, fielding calls from investors who were hearing rumors that I'd be backing out of Journey soon, or who were worried that we couldn't keep our employees on tight leashes.

For hours on end I'd reassured them and been busily texting Steven to make sure no one was cutting ties with us. I was more concerned about my employees than myself; luckily, Steven and I made plans early on for solid investment accounts if something went sideways.

When 8 p.m. finally hit I leaned back in my chair and sighed, catching a glimpse of my reflection in the window. My hair was a complete mess.

Mussed up and scruffy, not to mention the obvious stubble lining my jaw. As someone with dark hair, it only took a day for it to become noticeable.

Lacey shot me a text about half an hour ago to let me know that Rosie was tucked in. The empty plate from dinner that she snuck in earlier sat precariously on the corner of my desk.

I was lucky to have Lacey and smart enough to realize it. She was brilliant and it was crazy that she was *here*, with me.

Flicking off my desk light, leaving the room flooded with the glowing lights from the city, I stood and rolled my shoulders.

"Maybe I should get back into yoga..."

There was a light laugh and I jumped. Lacey stood in the doorway, which was open just enough to let her catch the remark.

"I'd like to see that," she said in a low, sultry voice.

Heat throbbed down to my loins. I tried to ignore it and gave her a half-smile.

"It does wonders for the body."

Stepping into the room, Lacey shut the door quietly behind her so as not to wake Rosie.

"And for the mind," she said seriously. "Here, sit down. You look tense."

I obliged, dropping into the office chair and wondering where this was going. She walked around behind me and my skin prickled when she dragged her hand up my upper arm, then gripped my shoulders on either side.

Expertly, she rolled and massaged the muscles there. At first I winced and tightened up. Lacey adjusted slightly and it felt like heaven, my muscles smoothing like butter under her fingers.

I groaned, head dropping forward. Her movements stopped for a moment, then started up again.

"Don't stop," I murmured as she worked her way slowly between my shoulder blades.

Every inch of my body was tingling like a livewire even as the tension melted away.

I heard her take a shaky breath and brought my head back up.

"Everything alright?" I asked, my voice coming out in a low rumble.

"Yeah." It came out in a breath, and I frowned, unsure if she was telling me the truth. In a steadier tone, she told me, "You need to relax more, Max. You're going to work yourself to death."

I couldn't help smiling at that. Mostly because it was true.

"It's all about balance."

"Mmm," I replied, dropping my head back and sliding down in the chair a bit. She reached around and, to my surprise, started lightly dragging her fingertips up my chest. I caught my breath; did she know what she was doing to me? "That's what the yoga's for."

"I never took you for the kind of guy to do yoga." There was a note of laughter in her voice, and I opened my eyes, our gazes locking immediately. Lacey bit her lip.

"There's a lot of things I can do with my body that would surprise you."

Where did that come from? As if I didn't know. It was impossible, agonizing, to have her touch me like this and not respond in some way.

In fact, if I wasn't careful, she was going to get a lot more than a verbal response. Conscious now of the stirring in between my legs, I shifted and tried to adjust myself. Lacey's gaze dropped and her fingers, now settled once again at my shoulders, stopped.

We both froze as it became obvious just how much her touch was affecting me. A lock of her hair, half-up in a messy bun, grazed my ear. My cock throbbed at the teasing sensation.

I was about to open my mouth and apologize when she pulled her hands away.

Great. Now I've destroyed a decade of friendship by falling apart like a horny teenager.

But, to my surprise, she didn't leave the room.

Instead Lacey walked around to the front of the chair, in the space between my legs and the desk. There wasn't a lot of room and her legs grazed my knees.

I waited for a response as her eyes stayed glued on my very obvious erection. The loose gym shorts did little to contain it. She swallowed and looked up at me quickly.

"You work yourself too hard," she said, taking deep, fast breaths. "I want to help you let go."

I was about to ask her what exactly she meant when she knelt between my legs.

It was hopeless. Just seeing her there was enough to almost finish me off.

"Lace," I said, reaching out quickly and covering one of her hands with my own, "you don't have to—I shouldn't have—"

She shook her head, turning her hand in mine and lacing our fingers together. Then unlacing them and gently pushing my hand away.

"I *want* to." Her eyes, in the dark, looked bright and dangerous.

Chapter 15

Lacey

Kneeling between Max's knees, two voices kept competing in my head:

This is insane. You're going to drive him away; he's going to think you're desperate.

And:

This isn't just for him; it's for both of you. You've never been so wet.

That last part was true. Just looking up at him from this position had my panties practically soaked through. I scooted forward on my knees, Max's legs spread wide on either side of me.

He was looking down at me with dark, serious eyes and a straight face. Business-like. It was oddly hot.

If he insisted again that I didn't have to do this, things would get awkward. But I gave it a few seconds and he didn't speak again, only watched me closely.

With almost-shaking fingers, I reached out and gripped the elastic waist of the workout shorts he had on. They did very, *very* little to hide how aroused he was right now.

And I was impressed.

Of course as a teen I'd snuck a few glances when we got out of the pool or when he stripped down to his boxers to change, but I never really had any idea how well-endowed Max was. Beneath the thin layer of fabric his cock rose stiff and ready, tenting the shorts in a way that looked painful.

I carefully pulled them off and down his legs, smiling as he struggled to not crush me. He was left in just his boxers and his t-shirt that fit well enough for me to see the defined muscles beneath.

The feeling of his body was what had gotten us here. His muscles were so tight and stiff, knotted… but even when they loosened it took everything in me not to trace the dips and cut edges.

Am I really doing this?

The thought went through my mind as I took in his boxer briefs. Slowly, I dragged my splayed hands back up his legs, enjoying the contrasting feel of his skin and hair. Smooth, rough, thigh muscles clenching under my touch.

He let out a choked breath as I reached the waistline of his boxers and gave them a little tug.

Gaining confidence, I looked up at him with a small, devilish smile. It was fun to toy with him and to have him on edge.

Max Munroe. Video game mogul, the man on magazine covers, a leader in the industry.

And he was putty in my hands.

I pulled the boxers down to his knees and watched his cock spring free. It was thicker than I'd imagined and the vein along the bottom thrummed with each beat of his heart. My mouth watered at the sight. Already I knew how smooth and hot that skin would feel under my tongue.

Licking my lips, I sat up further on my knees and hurriedly helped him peel the boxers away. Max's right hand ghosted over his balls and gave the base of his shaft a few quick pumps before making room for my hands. Looking up at him with a lustful intensity, I lightly played with his balls.

The skin immediately tightened up and he sucked in a breath.

I tried to hide my smile, leaning in further and giving the head of his cock a quick lick. Just a small one, but it was enough to taste the deliciousness of his skin. And I was right; he was smooth and hot. So tempting.

I gripped his thigh with one hand and his cock with the other, leaning over to push my lips around the tip. He sat up straight, bringing me in closer with a jerk of his hips as he gasped in surprise.

With an audible pop, I sat back and looked up at him with wide eyes.

"Too much? It's been a while…"

He shook his head, mussed hair brushing over his eyes as he pushed it away. "No, no." His mouth stayed open as if he didn't know what else to say.

When he didn't stop me physically or verbally, I slowly leaned down again and encircled the tip with my lips. Slipping down an inch, my tongue flicked the underside of the head. Then I licked again and sucked, feeling the thick vein throb against my bottom lip.

Losing myself now, I bobbed further down and let out an eager hum. He groaned and dropped his head back. He moved his hips upward, thrusting into my mouth lightly as I sucked and dragged my lips over his length, coating him in my spit.

I could feel the tension in his body all coiled, completely in this moment. With my left hand I grazed his balls and inner thighs, and with my right I kept a tight grip around the base of his cock. I could feel him getting harder by the moment, like hot silk and iron.

With a gasp I pulled back and took in my handiwork. Max's thick cock glistened in the dark and the head was swollen and darker. His legs were spread wide, hands gripping the arms of the chair and tendons standing out in his forearms.

The heated look he gave me was demanding. My lips parted. I wanted so badly for him to tell me what to do to him, what he wanted. I wanted to be commanded. I wanted to hear him use that voice he'd used at the office.

The one that warned not to disobey, or there'd be consequences.

...I wanted the consequences.

Squirming, I bit my lip and gave him a few quick pumps with a loose grip.

"Are you wet?" he asked in a low voice.

I nodded, feeling a gush of wet heat at my core. The sleep shorts I wore were very, very thin, a light green in color that was almost white. If I soaked through my panties, he'd see it. The thought made me flush with embarrassment and anticipation.

"Touch yourself."

My mouth dropped open in surprise. I was about to make an excuse, but he leaned forward and gripped my chin with one hand. His fingers held me there tightly, but not tight enough to hurt. His eyes bore into mine.

"Touch yourself while you suck me off."

I was breathing shallow and fast now, aware that it wouldn't take much at all to drive me over the edge. Not when he spoke to me like that.

Nodding, I leaned forward again and self-consciously slipped a hand into my shorts as I began to lick at the tip of his cock.

He huffed approvingly and sat back, eyes dragging over me.

I closed my own eyes and sucked the head of his cock into my mouth, circling my fingers once, firmly, around my clit as I did so.

It was almost too much and I shuddered. He made a sound, and when I opened my eyes he was staring down at me.

"Keep going," he demanded.

I bobbed down on his cock and felt it hit the back of my throat as a shock of pleasure went through my clit again. With a low moan, I found a steady pace and worked him further down my throat as I got myself off.

It wasn't hard. Years of being alone had taught me exactly what I liked, and I kept fingering my wet entrance shallowly, teasingly, before circling back to my clit. Each teasing stroke made me more and more tense, holding back less as I took more of his shaft into my mouth.

He was completely coated with my spit. When I ran a thumb over his balls again they were wet, almost as wet as my own fingers that I plunged repeatedly into my pussy.

As he filled my mouth, all I could think about was how badly I wanted him to fill the rest of me. How I wanted his cock to stretch me wide so I could feel the stinging burn of pleasure.

He threaded his fingers into my hair and gave it a light tug, guiding the pace as I sucked him off. Then he leaned forward and somehow managed to reach my pussy with his free hand, knocking my hand away.

His cock was deep in my throat now and all I could do was moan as he thrusted shallowly into me. It was almost suffocating, but I could breathe comfortably through my nose.

His fingers dipped into my slick center and quickly, effortlessly, he found my clit.

"Can you come like this?" he asked in a half-gasp, and through a haze of heightened senses I knew that he was losing it just as much as I was.

I hummed a response, trying to drag my lips up and down his cock as he pushed two fingers into me and found that delicious spot immediately.

With a low moan, I rocked my hips and rode his fingers, shuddering as an orgasm crashed over me. Max swore quietly, grip tightening in my hair as his own hips followed the same rhythm.

He pulled his fingers away and I whimpered. But then he was coming, the same hand he'd had buried in me moments ago now gripping my jaw again as he shot hot cum into my mouth. I tried to swallow it all, but some dribbled out the side of my lips and I licked at it with my tongue, the tip of his cock bouncing against my lower lip.

He swore again and gripped his cock by the base, smearing himself against my mouth like lipstick. I sat back, fingers buried inside my wet heat again as I came down from the orgasm, satisfied and borderline delirious.

In the dark, silent room, our eyes locked again.

Neither of us said anything. We were both content to just bask in the afterglow of something amazing that had been a long, *long* time coming.

Chapter 16

Lacey

If you asked me to create the perfect night from scratch, this would be it.

Watching old Disney movies with Rosie and Max, the two of us exchanging baffled looks at how insane some of the plot points seemed now that we were adults. Jasmine being lusted after by a full-grown man, Ariel selling her voice to follow a man around, the prince in Snow White stealing an unsolicited kiss.

"Let's hope she doesn't have an unhealthy obsession with any of this," he murmured as the two of us leaned over Rosie's reclining form. She was working hard, and failing, at keeping her eyes open.

I was working hard at trying to ignore his arm draped across the back of the couch. Every once in a while his fingers grazed by bare shoulder, and I had to fight back the bloom of heat at my core.

How was it possible to be turned on by something as silly as an accidental touch? Perhaps it was the very vivid memory of both of us getting off two nights ago only a few rooms away.

I bit my lip, zoning out as Mulan rocked that sad song right at the beginning of the film.

He had come home early, breezing through the door and looking particularly handsome. His outfit, simple jeans and a button-down, really suited him well. Not to mention his ass looked fantastic in those jeans.

I'd been distracted all afternoon to say the least. Enough so that I actually dropped a candle while trying to light it. I'd apologized profusely, cleaning it up and then immediately barricading myself in the bathroom with the excuse that I wanted to relax in the tub for a little while.

Only to be bombarded by texts from Kate.

Did you see Max on Miley & Dodd?

Did you hear what he SAID?

He's SEEING SOMEONE!?

He and Skylar are definitely not together?? Come on, Lace. How much clearer of a sign do you need?

I'd spent the next forty-five minutes ignoring the texts, wishing I'd tuned into the interview and jonesing for a glass of wine to try and calm down my aching nerves. I had a knot in my shoulders and kept startling at the smallest sounds.

But as the day went on, it was easy to grow comfortable around Max. Rosie's antics definitely helped, but in my heart I knew it also had to do with the fact that I had known him for forever. The only time I'd ever felt uncomfortable around him was when my secret crush on him was ready to burst at the seams.

I'd always managed to hold it back... until the other night.

I sighed and he looked at me over Rosie's curls.

"You okay?" he asked, a note of concern in his voice. "You falling asleep? We can call it a night?"

I plastered on a smile, hoping he couldn't read my mind right then.

"I'm fine. But this one on the other hand..."

I looked pointedly down at Rosie, who was now completely passed out. He made a strained face and carefully extricated his arm from around the two of us, leaving me feeling cold.

He gave me a "shush" motion with one hand pressed against his lips—*damn, don't think about those lips*—and carefully scooped her into his arms. Rosie groaned, but only readjusted and buried herself into his shoulder.

I watched him pad toward the hallway barefoot in his sweatpants, a smile on my face, before getting up and following.

Leaning against the wall between the bathroom and Rosie's room, I could hear him murmur a goodnight to his daughter. He shut the door quietly behind him and gave me a tired smile.

This is how it should be all the time, I thought. Rosie falling asleep in her dad's arms. Spending amazing, quality time together.

He sighed, running a hand through his hair. "We should probably get to sleep too," he half-whispered. "I've gotta get back to work tomorrow and I'm sure you're exhausted after putting up with us."

I gave him a nudge and a silly grin. "I'll put up with you two any day. Happily."

Something in his face shifted at my words, and I tensed, wondering if I'd said the wrong thing. Was I getting too attached?

Before I could overthink it Max leaned in and gave me a light kiss on the cheek.

I leaned up on tip toes and boldly pressed my lips to his.

Soft and sweet, and I hoped that he could feel how grateful I was in it. Just to be here and to be included in his life.

I gave him a small, quick smile and turned, heading for my bedroom.

Holding my breath.

Chapter 17

Max

I sauntered into the office the next day feeling relaxed and content. The half-day I'd taken off work after the interview had been perfect; I couldn't have scripted it better. Lounging on the couch with Lacey and Rosie curled up next to me, watching movies and eating an entire bag of popcorn and so many chocolate chip cookies. I'll have to admit to quite a bit of daydreaming about the next time Lacey and I were alone together.

It was all too good to be true.

Tara's eyes gave it away when I reached the fourth floor.

"Everything okay?" I asked warily.

No way could there be a leak so soon after the interview. If there was one, whoever the culprit was, was ballsy.

"I'm not sure," she replied evasively, holding out a newspaper.

I felt eyes on my back as I took it and prayed it wasn't anything too damaging. With a frown, I flipped the paper open.

Shit. Bottom right corner of the front page. A photo of Lacey, Rosie and I out on a walk. Only a few days ago, we'd gone to a park for about an hour after Rosie got out of school, then I'd come straight back to the office.

I felt a rise of anger, veins pulsing as I looked at the photo. In it I wore my casual work clothes and Lacey had on a flowy pink top and jeans. She looked great, no doubt about that, and was laughing at something. It was a good photo.

But I wanted to keep her to myself.

They had no right to paste her on the front page like this.

The headline was small, but in bold font: **Who's Stealing Max Munroe's Heart?**

When I looked up Tara sat back in her chair. Her expression was a mix of regret at having shown me and slight fear.

"At the news stand?" I asked.

She nodded, but then added, "Aisha dropped it off. She wants to talk to you when you have a second."

Without a word, I turned on my heel and headed straight for her office, work bag still slung over my shoulder. It wasn't Aisha or Tara's fault that the media was so invasive, but I was pretty ticked off at having my personal life constantly splashed all over the paper.

Aisha had a nice office, a decent size, with a window that let in a flood of light. She looked grim when I stepped in with a cursory knock.

"You saw it?" she asked, turning her chair to face me.

"Yeah. Is there anything we can do to stop this kind of thing from happening?"

My PR rep gave me a hard look. "Max, you said on air the other day that there was *someone special* in your life. Are you really surprised this appeared the day after?"

I took a deep breath through my nose, not wanting to admit that I was at fault. "They have no right to take photos of just anyone and put them on the cover—"

"What do you want to do, sue them?"

I snapped my mouth shut, considering if that was possible. Aisha rolled her eyes.

"Look, I know we had that conversation the other day, and I'm happy you found someone you care about. But I need a little clarification here. Is she really your nanny?"

Outraged with my mouth open, I looked at the newspaper still gripped in my hands.

"It says that? How would they even know that?"

"You didn't read it? Apparently she's been spotted *out and about* with Rosie quite a bit. But no one cares about the nanny until it turns into a tryst, and judging from that photo it's not a longshot to see how they came to that conclusion. So, do you and your nanny have a thing?"

"She's not my nanny," I said through gritted teeth. "Not really. She's an old friend, helping out until I can find a replacement."

"For Ann?" Aisha asked in surprise. "It's been a few months. Have you not been interviewing?"

I looked guiltily at my feet. I hadn't posted the job yet. And I had zero excuses.

"Did you even ask Tara to start looking?"

I rolled my eyes at her. "Tara is my assistant for Journey, not my personal life."

"Maybe you should think about hiring an assistant for your personal life, pronto. You really shouldn't be surprised with all the attention," Aisha scoffed. "I don't know what to tell you, Max, except that if you *do* want to keep this private you should find a new nanny immediately. And stop baiting talk show hosts."

I glared at her. It was rare that I gave Aisha an attitude. She'd earned my respect a long time ago and was careful to mind the boundaries I put up.

"Or you could drop her," she said in a flat voice that made it clear she meant business. "Those are your options. Consider them. I can't do anything about that right now, so you'll have to deal with it. *Apocalypse* releases in a week, so let's keep it together until then."

She gave a little wave gesture to indicate that we were done as her phone rang. Trying to keep a lid on my frustration, I headed down the hallway and toward my office. Victor was in the break room leaning up against the counter and chatting away with one of the designers. Our eyes met as I passed, and I saw a flash of glee in them.

The one good thing about the article was that it would only solidify the fact that under no circumstances could he go anywhere near Lacey. She was off limits.

"Thanks for the heads up," I said to Tara shortly, tossing the newspaper in the trash. Later, when I had time to calm down, I'd apologize and thank her properly.

It wasn't a great start to the morning. That was Murphy's law, though, wasn't it? Last night was so wonderful and I felt so close to Lacey.

The soft look in her eyes as she closed the gap between us and pressed her mouth to mine had carried me right through this morning. I hadn't slept most of the night, content to stay up and replay all the sweet and sexy parts of the last few days, wondering when they would happen again.

I barely sat down at my desk when it hit me: Lacey didn't know about the article.

I couldn't let her wander out into the world and see it with no warning. Standing up almost immediately, I strode through the door and told Tara, "I'll be back soon."

The elevator ride down to the lobby was tense. I ignored the glances of my employees and dug my phone out of my pocket, pulling up Lacey's name and tapping the call button as I stepped through the front doors and into the sunlight.

It rang but she didn't pick up.

8 a.m. She was probably getting Rosie on the bus.

Pacing the length of the building twice, I impatiently dialed again. It rang. No answer.

Should I text her? Somehow that seemed too casual for this situation. Maybe she wouldn't be as upset as I was, though.

Who was I kidding. At this very moment she might be getting odd looks from parents and nannies, and have no idea why.

"Hey, Max," Victor called from the doorway of Journey Studios. "We have a meeting with marketing in a few minutes. You can't miss this one." He was a little too smug for my liking and my shoulders tensed.

"I'll be there in a minute," I ground out, trying not to slay him with my eyes.

He didn't move from the doorway. "Aisha told me not to show up without you, so..."

Taking a deep breath, I tried to stifle my growing anxiety. A quick glance at the phone; no text or call back from Lacey.

Where could she be?

"Alright," I relented, turning toward the building. "I'm coming."

It was going to be a long day.

Later on, after way too many meetings, I marched through the door of the apartment and scoured the main area.

Some of Lacey's things were here and there. A pair of her shoes near the door, a cardigan hung on the back of a chair. Her laptop out on the coffee table.

Seeing them calmed me, but just barely.

Walking through the apartment, I called out, "Lace?"

My phone was clutched in my hand. I'd tried to call her a few more times throughout the busy day and hadn't gotten an answer.

When I reached the hallway, I could hear the water on in the bathroom. She must be showering. My shoulders dropped and I turned toward the kitchen.

Then paused.

There was a blazer hanging on the coat rack, one I'd never seen before. With a frown I pulled on the hem. It was stylish and minimalistic, a trendy camel color.

Uh-oh. Skylar wasn't in my bathroom, was she…?

I only had to wait a few more tense minutes to find out. The door opened and Lacey stepped out, wrapped in a terrycloth robe. She saw me and jumped, a hand pressed to her chest.

"Oh! You startled me." Her eyes darted to the clock above the stove. "You're early, aren't you? Is everything okay?"

She sounded skeptical as she padded out into the living area, toweling her hair dry lazily. Her glasses were off and she squinted at me with a smile.

"We need to talk," I said bluntly, nerves suddenly flooding my system. Rosie was at a friend's house so I knew it would be safe to talk without her hearing.

No way she'd seen the article, or she wouldn't be so casual right now. I'd had all day to think about how to break the awkward news that *we* were news, and still hadn't figured out how I was going to say it.

She paused, the towel dropping to her side. "Okay…"

"Why didn't you pick up today?" This morning's anxiety flooded through me again. The marketing meeting had been a nightmare, with Victor arguing that we should be putting more focus on foreign markets and Aisha arguing right back while shooting me concerned glances.

Lacey quirked an eyebrow. "Um. I was a little busy. Rosie was late, so I had to get hold of Gerald and have him drive us—"

"I texted and asked you to call me when you were free."

I didn't mean for it to come out so blunt, and her expression hardened. She put her hands on her hips and narrowed her eyes at me.

"I'm not always free, Max. And I'm sorry I missed your text, I spent all morning running around."

Illogically, my brain took the conversation off the rails. "So what would happen if there was an emergency?" The article was *not* an emergency, but now I couldn't stop myself. "What if there was an accident or something happened with Rosie and I needed you—"

Her face fully shut down. I'd ignored the warning signs and now she was upset.

"I know I agreed to help you out, but I like to think you'd trust me enough to take care of things if there was an emergency. I'm not going to be free every second of the day to be at your beck and call."

Her voice was hard and cold, her posture stiff. I opened my mouth to apologize, but nothing came out. My fists were clenched at my side as I tried to untangle the mess I'd made.

"It doesn't matter," she said after an agonizingly drawn-out moment of silence. "We do need to talk. I found another job. I was at a job interview earlier, that's why I didn't pick up."

Her chin tilted upward as she said the words and they hit me right in the gut.

"Wh—Lace, what?"

"I didn't want to tell you like this, but I think the lines are getting a little blurred here. I was fine with helping out but I'm not your minion. I let them know I'll need two weeks, and I can help you look for nannies, but after that..."

She trailed off, eyes dropping to the ground. It felt like all the air had gone out of me. I stood there, deflated and confused. There was a whole train of questions running through my mind.

Found a job? Didn't she already have a job to go back to? I was hesitant to ask the question because I could tell she was super uncomfortable about her work situation.

"Okay," I finally said, at a loss for any other response. "Okay. Well, congratulations, I guess." I shoved my hands in my pockets.

We stood staring at one another. The moment felt oddly empty.

"I'm sorry," she said, clutching the damp towel to her chest. "I really wanted to find another way to tell you…"

"No," I shook my head. "I get it. I'm sorry if this was all too much. We can talk about it tomorrow. I should—"

What? Go back to the office? Pretend I had another interview to do?

Lacey turned toward the hallway, probably wanting to put some clothes on instead of standing in a robe in the living room. I turned away, and grabbed a light jacket off the coat rack, now understanding what the nice blazer had been for.

Outside it was beautiful and sunny. Traffic was light. A curly-haired dog bounced happily toward me with its owner.

As I started to walk with no particular destination in mind, I realized how horrid I felt *inside*. Like I was losing Lacey all over again.

Chapter 18

Lacey

When Max came out of his bedroom the next morning, he looked exhausted.

Guilt swallowed me and I wanted to just disappear. Rosie was already on the bus and about an hour into school. I wasn't quite sure why he was still home but didn't want to stress him out by asking.

Especially since I didn't even know if we were talking at this point.

He wandered out in basketball shorts and a t-shirt, giving me a sad smile.

"I started coffee," I said, clutching my own cup and staring at my open book without reading a word.

Yesterday had been an accident.

I hadn't meant to spill the news so soon. Not the way it came out, anyway. The interview had been a surprise—a last minute call and I'd hurried off to it as soon as Rosie was on the bus. It'd been a little over an hour long and I found myself chatting pleasantly with the director and exchanging ideas.

By the time I'd left it was almost 10 a.m. and I was buoyed by the feeling that it had gone well. Really well.

But my guilt leaked in all around the edges; I'd taken a bus to the interview, not wanting to tip Gerald off with where I was going or how I was dressed. The casual business attire had been a panicked, last-minute buy the day before with Kate for moral support.

When are you going to tell him? she'd asked as I smoothed the blazer and new white blouse down over my abdomen.

I have no idea.

I mean, Kate had said, smiling a pained smile, *at least he'll be happy you're staying in Cold Springs.*

But I hadn't gotten that detail out when I told him I found a job.

He'd caught me off guard the night before, barging into the apartment and demanding to know where I'd been and why I hadn't answered. There were a lot of other things I hadn't told him that had thrown yesterday off, not just the job interview.

With a sigh, he sat down across from me. He looked a little grim, but also a little apologetic. Those caramel eyes had that puppy-dog look to them, the same look he always got when he knew he'd done something wrong.

"Hey. I'm sorry about yesterday. I was really stressed out."

I waved it off, trying not to clutch my book so tightly.

"It's fine. I'm sorry I dropped the bomb on you like that. I really wanted to just...talk."

There was a moment of silence, and then, with another sigh, he said, "So let's talk now."

"Okay."

Where to start?

"You were serious," he stated rather than asked. "About finding a new job?"

I nodded, and he mirrored the movement, brows knit.

"Alright. I understand. But can I ask... I thought you *had* a job? At Pratt?"

I took a deep breath, knowing it was finally time to spill. To push away the embarrassment and finally tell the truth.

"I did. But right before you asked me to come out here, I actually got let go. The library got a new director and he... kind of canned me."

His eyebrows rose and he leaned in. "Oh, Lace. I'm so sorry. And, I get why you didn't want to bring it up, but I wish you'd been comfortable enough to tell me."

I let out a big breath. "I know. I'm sorry about that, I think I needed to get used to the idea before I told anyone. Only Kate knew; my mom doesn't even know."

I bit my lip at the mention of my mother. But Max knew me too well and could still see right through me.

"Is everything okay with her?" he asked carefully.

I took a second to be grateful for the fact that he was letting the whole job thing go so easily. I knew we weren't done talking about it yet, but part of me had been afraid that he'd be angry, offended, or accuse me of leaving him in the lurch.

"Actually," I said, feeling the worry start gnawing at me again, "I'm not sure. She had an accident yesterday, her neighbor called to tell me. She's in the hospital."

He half-stood, letting go of his coffee, his eyes wide. "Do you need to go? I can have Gerald drive you, or buy you a plane ticket—"

I couldn't help smiling at his show of helpfulness. She only lived two hours away, so a plane ticket was a bit much.

"No, no. I called the hospital yesterday and they said she's stable and doing okay. She fell and broke her hip. But she has lots of friends checking in and visiting." The call had been a shock, coming on my walk back to Skyside. And then it set in just how old my mom had gotten. She'd been so independent for years that I didn't think of it often, but she was in her seventies now.

"I'm going to give her a call in a bit." I glanced at the clock. "Once I'm sure she's up and has eaten and everything. I want to hear it from her, and make sure she doesn't need me out there."

He nodded slowly, dropping into his seat. "Well let me know if she needs anything. There are some great facilities around here, and some great surgeons too. I'm happy to get her up here."

I smiled at him and reached across the expanse, taking his hand. "Thank you. I'm sure it'll be fine, but I'll let you know."

We sat in silence for a few minutes, both of us lost in thought and sipping our coffee. My heart ached at the thought at having to leave, and as if reading my mind, he said, "Rosie will be crushed."

He had visibly deflated. I felt guilty again, but...

"I'll still be here, in Cold Springs. Once I find somewhere I can afford." I laughed a little self-deprecatingly. Actually, I had some savings and could get a mid-level apartment, but I needed to make sure my new salary would sustain it.

Max blinked at me in surprise with a big smile on his face. "You know you can always stay here."

All the breath went out of me. The offer was very tempting.

I let it sink in, and my heart dropped as I realized it was impossible. Staying here would be amazing. I'd love to get up and see Rosie every day, spend time with Max when I got home from work.

I swallowed. A part of me, a large part, knew that it couldn't be. My feelings for him had gone beyond my comfort zone. It was hard to keep them in check after what we'd shared, and already I'd had a lot of *what if* thoughts.

He didn't need his life getting any more complicated.

"Thank you," I said warmly, not wanting to say "no" right away and offend him. "I'll let you know."

We smiled tentatively at one another. There was still a lot to talk about—but I needed to sort things out with my mom and tie up some loose ends with the hiring process. In two weeks I'd start as the Research Librarian at Mabel Humphrey Library. A dream job, one that felt like fate.

He got up and grabbed a newspaper out of his work bag. "I've got something I need to show you. It's the reason I was trying so hard to get a hold of you yesterday." He handed me the paper and I saw the picture of the three of us on the front. Oh my, the press was trying to make us a couple…

Things had definitely just become more complicated…

Chapter 19

Lacey

"Hey, mom. How are you doing?"

I waited with bated breath, listening for the tone of voice that would tell me how she was *really* doing.

"Oh, I'm fine sweetheart!"

I let the breath out.

"Moira called me yesterday, she said you fell down the front steps?"

Mom huffed, the sound of her restlessly shuffling around in a hospital bed coming through the line. "You know those steps, they've been crumbling for years. I just happened to catch my shoe on the wrong spot and took a tumble. Not a big deal."

You're in a hospital, I wanted to point out, *a few days away from a major surgery.*

"Do you want me to come down there?" I asked. "I'm not too far away—I'm actually up in Cold Springs."

"Cold Springs! What are you doing there?"

"I came out here to help a friend initially. But, I actually just took a new job here."

Unfortunately, mom knew me well and could tell that I was being evasive. She always had my number.

"Mmhmm. Which friend were you helping out?"

I waited a beat, and then confessed: "Max. He needed someone to watch his daughter while he found a new nanny."

"And how *is* Maxwell doing?"

I bit my tongue, remembering that tone she'd always taken on when it came to me and Max. Growing up even my mom had acted like there was something between us. Maybe she was a little right, at least half-right, later on but it wasn't something I enjoyed hearing as a pre-teen or when I'd been dating Craig.

"He's doing well," I replied lightly, hoping she wouldn't dig too much on the subject.

As always, mom exceeded my expectations and dove right in.

"Well I can't say I'm surprised, Lacey. I always said you two were meant for each other, and—"

I tried to tune her out, leaning against the kitchen island with a half-finished shopping list in front of me. But the longer she spoke about having seen the "spark" between us years ago, the hotter my cheeks got. Finally, I couldn't take it anymore.

"Mom, I know you feel like you had a hunch about this, but we were just friends." The scoff on the other line told me that she definitely did not believe that. "And I wasn't calling to talk about *my* personal life or Max's. I was calling to see if you wanted me there. For your surgery and everything you're dealing with."

She laughed, a tinkling, light sound that was actually more reassuring than her verbally saying she was fine.

Once again, mom threw me for a loop.

"You don't have to worry about that, sweetheart. I have Jim here with me."

My mind went blank. Jim? Who was Jim? I asked as much, and she replied, "Oh, a man I've been seeing. He's the one who drove me to the hospital you know. He'll be here for the surgery and drive me home, too."

"Don't worry, Lacey, I'll look after her!" a muffled voice with a slight southern accent called in the background.

I stared across the room, trying to process this on top of everything else that had been dropped on me for the last few days.

Max and I had some very interesting turns in our relationship, I'd cut short my temporary job as Rosie's nanny and accepted my dream job, my mom was in the hospital after a bad fall, and she was *dating*.

"So, is Jim, uh, serious?" I ventured.

Mom dropped her voice, but probably not enough for Jim not to catch her words. "Well, we'll see how it goes… we've only been seeing each other for a few months, but now with my surgery we'll be roommates for a bit! He's moving in to help me out during the recovery."

"That's great," I spilled out, partly meaning it and partly still shocked by the news.

"Maybe now that you're closer, you can come and visit," mom said warmly. The surprise started to wear off as I heard in her voice how much she missed me. I missed her, too.

"Yes! Definitely!" I meant it. "Soon—as soon as you're settled back home. I'd like to meet Jim." Oddly, I meant that too. As much as I missed my dad, it was good to know that my mom was taken care of and not alone. "Can you keep me updated about the surgery? When it'll be?"

"Of course, sweetheart. And if you're okay with it, I'll give Jim your number. That way he can catch you up the day of, too."

I agreed and we slipped into easy conversation as she told me about the shared room they'd initially put her in and how her roommate kept purposely peeing on the floor. Now she was comfortable in a single occupant room and was going into surgery in two days, if everything worked out. Somehow, she was incredibly positive and upbeat.

"It's the drugs," she whispered slyly. "They really load you up if you ask, especially at my age."

I laughed and made her promise again to keep in touch as the next few days passed. Jim called out a goodbye from somewhere in the background, and I decided I liked his southern accent.

With a sigh, I hung up and sat back. At least I had the whole day ahead of me to process.

A little after 2 p.m. Skylar, in all her splendor, stopped by to pick up Rosie for a few nights away.

Before they left, Rosie turned around in the doorway and ran to hug me. "You'll be here when I get back?" she asked, peering up at me with her dad's big brown eyes. Ever since breaking the news to her that I'd be moving out and starting a new job soon, she'd been particularly attached to me.

"Of course." I smiled and ruffled her curls. Skylar gave me an appraising look before taking Rosie's hand and heading for the elevator.

I took a luxuriously long nap and then did a bit of self-care, including a hot shower and skincare routine. The scent of lavender helped my body relax and wash away the last few days of stress.

Wandering out of the bathroom in my robe, I tried to figure out what to make for dinner. There wasn't much in the fridge. I probably should've made time to go shopping, but too late now.

The penthouse door rattled and I jumped. Max stepped in and froze when he saw me in the kitchen.

"Oh," I breathed with a small laugh. "It's you! I wasn't expecting you early again. Would've sent you to the grocery store if I knew."

He kept his eyes on me as walked down the hallway after tossing his work bag to the side.

"Skylar pick up Rosie?" he asked casually. But I caught the flicker of his gaze over my hips and legs, realizing at the last second that my right thigh was almost entirely exposed. I tried to tuck the robe around my legs with a little cough.

"Yeah, everything went well."

"Good. You had time to talk to your mom?"

I nodded and filled him in on everything. The impending surgery, my mom's great attitude, and Jim.

"Jim?" he repeated, a confused look on his face.

"That's what I was thinking, too, but he actually sounds like a nice guy. I might go down for a day or two once she's home and make sure everything's okay."

"Of course, just let me know what you need. I can have Gerald pick Rosie up from school and drop her at the office, plus we can use the babysitter in between. No big deal."

"Thanks," I said honestly, giving him a small nudge with my shoulder. We sat side by side in comfortable silence. With memories of the day slowly spinning out in my mind, I smiled slowly.

"You won't believe what she said," I murmured, "once she found out I was here."

"Was she upset?" Max asked, brow cocked. A ridiculous question since my mom had always loved him.

"Of course not. She was a little too happy about it, actually." Maybe it was the couple of glasses of wine I'd had lazing around the apartment, but I spilled it. "She's still insisting that we're meant for each other after all these years. Didn't seem surprised at all that I was in Cold Springs."

He smiled a slow smile but didn't laugh as I did. I quieted, my eyes meeting his.

Without another word he leaned forward and pressed his lips to mine.

His kiss was heart-stopping. I held my breath, then kissed him back, pressing into it. He tasted like fresh air and mint. His hand snuck around my lower back and pulled me closer aggressively, the stool scraping across the tiles.

The lights overhead were dim and, once again, all my senses were alive as the kiss deepened. His fingers lightly massaged my back through the thin terrycloth robe and I found myself slipping closer to him on the stool.

My own arm wrapped under his, knees falling apart to get closer. His other hand grazed my thigh and I gasped into the kiss.

"Is this okay?" he rumbled, that deep voice I loved so much. I nodded, kissed him again.

He gently grabbed my thigh and rubbed his thumb over it lazily, making goosebumps appear. When he pulled back for a moment I made a sound of longing and he smiled.

"Here," he said, slowly moving away and standing, offering me his hand. "Let's get a little more comfortable."

I stood and followed as he walked backward. For a moment it looked like he was going toward the living area, but I glanced at the hallway and gave him a tug in that direction. He followed me, no hesitation.

We started down the hall, our fingers still intertwined.

I'd been in his room a few times to grab things quickly or toss his laundry in the wash, but never like this. Never naked on top of the comforter, turning to look at him in the glowing light of the city pooling through the windows.

Taking a deep breath, he stepped closer and wrapped his arms around me. He held me as if I were breakable and I couldn't help grinning before pressing a more insistent kiss to his lips.

Luckily, he was always a quick learner. All it took was pulling back teasingly a few times for him to cup the back of my head and capture my lips. There was a hint of dominance in the way he tightened his grip around my waist and I shivered.

No longer questioning, he slipped a hand beneath my robe, his fingertips moving along my waist and upwards. He grazed the underside of my breast.

"Max," I gasped, arching my back into his touch instinctively. He smiled against my lips and tweaked a nipple, making wet heat pool between my legs instantly.

Exhilarated, I tugged him toward the bed, fumbling with the buttons on his shirt. I managed to undo a couple before he stripped it off effortlessly, tossing it to the side. Taking a moment to run my eyes over his body, I felt such a longing for him, all of him. Right now.

That dark hair, those caramel eyes glinting in the dark, and the abs of a god, my mind was racing with all the things I wanted to do to him.

He wasted no time in undoing the tie around my waist and stripping the robe off, immediately dropping to his knees. I sat on the edge of the bed and he pressed my legs apart determinedly, making me gasp again. But he changed course and buried his head in my breasts and started kissing. Then licking. Sucking. Biting lightly until I was softly groaning and squirming. I was so hungry for him.

When I couldn't take it any longer I buried my hands in his hair, tugged lightly, and begged, "*Please*."

As if I'd said the magic word, he stood—his arousal more than evident in how it pressed insistently against his pants—and started to undo his belt.

I licked my lips, watching as he flicked open the button of his jeans and shucked them off. His boxer briefs were straining and I couldn't wait any more. With one swift movement I tugged them down, watching as his cock bounced before me.

With a gentle push he had me splayed out on the bed. I held my breath as he climbed over my body, muscles shifting with each movement, cock bobbing heavily between my legs. The closer he got to my core the wetter I became.

Finally he stopped and sat on his knees. His eyes dropped to my pussy, taking in the sight of just how badly I wanted him. With one hand he gripped the base of his shaft, balancing himself on the bed with the other. He gave himself two quick strokes and then leaned forward, carefully swiping the head up my soaked slit and coating it.

He gripped my thighs and pulled me close and continued to tease my entrance. I could feel my desire dripping down my thighs now and threw my head back, moaning. "Please, Max. I need you." He slowly pushed into me. It had been so long that for a moment his girth stretched me uncomfortably but my body happily adjusted, tightening around him. A shiver of electricity shot up my spine to my nipples and I couldn't help reaching up to cup my own breasts with another moan.

He swore quietly, bracing himself over me now that he filled me to the hilt. Slowly, he began to pump in and out, making sure to press in as far as he could before drawing out almost entirely. The delicious pace and overwhelming sensation of his cock stretching me wide with each stroke had me panting in minutes.

Wanting more, I wrapped my legs around his hips and tried to pull him deeper. Max stuttered out a groan and dropped to one elbow, picking up the pace. He moved smoothly, the new angle brushing my clit with his hard abs on each stroke.

"Just like that," I murmured, burying my fingers in his hair again. I wanted to be his; I was *finally* his, right now, as he pumped into me, filling me completely and creating this amazing burn through my whole body. It was like being on fire.

"Come for me," he demanded breathlessly, voice hoarse as his lips dragged over my skin.

I moaned and tilted my hips to meet his as the pace grew faster, my clit throbbing and muscles tightening as the orgasm took over.

The sparks turned into a blissful whiteout as waves of pleasure resonated through my entire body. I lost control of my limbs, legs going limp and nails digging into his scalp as he continued to pound into me. He raised his hips to come in at a different angle, his own breath ragged as I chanted his name over and over again.

Just as I started to spiral down deliciously from my high, he found his. With a groan he came, hips snapping against my thighs as his cock pulsed deep inside. I tightened my legs around him again and held him close until he slowed, breathless and sated.

Both of us fell limp onto the mattress. We were both sweaty and it felt oh-so good. He turned on his side and stretched an arm across my waist.

I wriggled closer, pressing my hip against his lower abdomen and purred happily. I was right where I belonged.

Chapter 20

Max

Steven popped into my office as I was busy reading through the final reports on presales and manufacturer output for *Apocalypse Summit*. Shipments had gone out the night before, when I'd been fast asleep with Lacey in my bed.

I was eternally grateful for Skylar right now. She'd freed up a few days. A few days of bliss...

Lacey and I hadn't talked yet about last night. But then things with Lacey rarely needed words.

Still, I wanted to be intentional. So I tried to bang out the last few necessary items on my list to free up the rest of the day for trying to figure out what I wanted to say to her when I got home.

Stay here, with Rosie and me.

Take off your clothes and get back in my bed.

Do you have any regrets about last night?

I knew that, on my end at least, I didn't regret a thing. Actually, part of me was thinking that it had all worked out perfectly. Yes, I'd harbored a heavy crush on Lacey for years. Literally over a decade. But somehow it felt like it had all come together last night exactly how it was supposed to.

If we'd gotten together as teenagers, it would've been a fumbling mess.

And it was Lacey.

Not just anyone.

Of course I lost myself to her quickly, overwhelmed by all of it. The feel of her breasts dragging against my bare chest, the sounds she made, the tight wet heat of her—

I snapped back to reality, trying to focus on Steven in the doorway.

"You're not going to believe this," he said in that quiet, serious tone that immediately told me something big would follow.

I sat up straight, expecting a bombshell. Another attack on my personal life, another leak, a huge financial loss.

Instead, he said, "We found the files and encrypted emails to a third-party contact at the Underground. It all came from Jake's personal laptop."

My mind went blank and a rushing sound filled my ears. I dropped the papers in my hand. Steven stepped fully into the room, closing the door behind him.

Out in the hallway I saw the elevators open and security step out.

"I took the liberty of calling them," he said with a nod in their direction. "They'll be removing him right now, unless you disagree."

I shook my head, my brain still trying to catch up.

"Jake...?"

But he wasn't involved in the design of the game itself. He was just Victor's assistant.

Steven nodded solemnly. "Gregory," the head IT guy, "came into my office right after you got here."

"I don't get it though. How...? If it was on his personal laptop?"

With a sigh, he crossed his legs. "Turns out Jake isn't as smart as he looks. He made copies of the files and had those on his work computer. Then emailed them to his personal email. He logged on to our server from his personal computer to send the emails to the contact, and that's how IT found it. But it took them a while to dig it all up."

I shook my head, disbelieving. "I was expecting one of the developers, honestly, or maybe an intern."

"Me too," he confessed. "Either way, I'm happy we figured it out. Can send him on his way. As an added bonus, Victor will be embarrassed as all hell. Remember how hard he advocated for Jake?"

A slow, small smile stretched my mouth. It would be good to get one up on Victor.

At that moment I made a big decision. I was going to step down. I was done with this level of drama. I had put my time in and created a top-tier powerhouse gaming company and now I'd let someone else deal with the tough stuff. I was serious about it this time and I wasn't going to change my mind.

"I'm going to retire."

He blinked as he stared across the desk at me. The words sank in and his eyes widened.

"Retire… from the industry?" he asked, unsure of which direction I was going.

I shook my head. "No. I don't think I could ever stop completely, but these last few years have been unhealthy. And I don't enjoy that piece of it anymore. I want to spend time with Rosie and—" I almost said Rosie and Lacey, but caught myself. "—and get back to what matters," I finished lamely.

Steven saw right through me. He pursed his lips.

Everyone on the floor looked up as Jake was literally dragged toward the elevators, his youthful face twisted with outrage. Behind them Victor was jogging to keep up and speaking loudly. His eyes were wide and as surprised as everyone else's.

It would be good to take him down a notch, but now that I was coming to terms with leaving Journey to focus on my life, the idea of revenge or public embarrassment just wasn't that appealing.

"We should set up a time to go over all this, especially with legal, and I'll get an outside lawyer too. But I think I want to make Journey's stocks public. And sell my own shares, privately, at a low price. Leave the decision making in the hands of the fans."

He looked impressed. "Okay, I see where you're going with this. But, yeah, you should meet with an unbiased lawyer first. I think it's a good move though; this way control goes to a board and not directly to your successor." He glanced through the glass windows at Victor, who was standing outside the closed elevator doors, completely baffled.

With a sigh I shuffled the papers around, making sure everything was signed and reviewed. When I looked up, Steven was grinning at me.

"Kate will be happy to hear that you two idiots finally came around," he said smugly, letting me know that my near-slip hadn't gone unnoticed. "Tell Lacey I said hi."

Chapter 21

Lacey

Breathless, I let myself into the penthouse and immediately dropped my heavy duffle bag. I'd overpacked, but wasn't sure how long I'd stay at mom's. Luckily what she'd told me over the phone was true—the surgery had gone well, even if she had a long road to recovery, and Jim was watching over her carefully.

I'd spent two days with her and Jim, who thoughtfully slept at his own house and only visited during the day when I was there. He was a nice guy, not exactly what I pegged as my mom's type, but they seemed to really care about each other. He frequently smiled indulgently at her and teased her in a slow southern drawl. It was easy to see why she was so happy, despite weeks and weeks of physical therapy and healing in her future.

But it was good to be back in Cold Springs. It felt odd to think that, but it was true. I could sleep easier now knowing that mom was fine. And I had a few more days to tidy up before I started at Mabel Humphrey Library. Most of that time would be spent searching for my replacement.

The sound of heels tapping on the tile floor made me frown. It was an out-of-place sound for the penthouse, unless Rosie was playing dress-up...

I turned just inside the door and saw Skylar walking purposely toward me. She wore a pencil skirt, a completely open blouse, heels, and a lace bra. Her long hair was flowing down her back. Dark lips pursed, she barely glanced at me.

"I have to go," she said, grabbing a purse off the bench and slinging it over her shoulder, "but tell Max I said thanks for last night."

With a smirk over her shoulder, she stepped into the hallway, buttoning her shirt.

The door closed behind her, and I stared at the place she'd stood only moments before.

What was Skylar doing here…? Max hadn't mentioned her coming by to pick up Rosie or…whatever she was here for. My heart sank as dark thoughts ran through my mind, images I didn't want to conjure up, but in they came.

I turned and stalked down the hallway, throat tight and eyes burning as I fought back confused tears.

Just as I reached the kitchen, Max rounded the corner out of the hallway. He was shirtless and in low-slung sweatpants.

"Hey," he greeted, perking up when he noticed me. "You're back—I wasn't sure if you were staying another day or two."

"Me either," I replied, my voice flat as I took in his mussed-up appearance.

He paused, frowning, and took a carton of almond milk out of the fridge. "Everything okay?" he asked. "Your mom good? You look a little upset."

I stayed standing, trying to fight back the lump in my throat.

"Yeah," I said breathlessly. "Just ran into Skylar. In the hallway. She said to tell you thanks for last night."

He froze, about to pour the milk into a bowl of granola.

"What?" he asked dumbly.

I wanted to laugh, but knew it would come out sounding anxious and crazy. Swallowing it back, I shrugged. "Pretty straight forward if you ask me. From what I gathered, she stayed here last night."

His eyes searched mine, then darted to my hand where it clenched the back of the stool. His eyes widened in realization.

"Lacey, you don't think... you know I'd never..."

I waited, my blood running cold. He put down the carton of milk and circled the island, stepping close and taking my elbow.

"I'd never do that to you." His voice was soft and quiet, brow furrowed as he tried to catch my eyes. But the worried tears were about to spill over and I didn't want him to see. "Skylar missed her flight out of town last night when she dropped Rosie off late. I told her she could sleep here—on the couch."

He stepped to the side and gestured.

The couch was obviously rumpled, a quilt from the closet bunched up and a pillow at the other end. My breathing slowed down to a reasonable pace as I took it in.

"Hey," he said seriously, righting me so that our eyes finally met. "I'm sorry; she's trying to get under your skin. She knows I..."

He trailed off, now the one unable to look me in the eye.

"She knows what?" I asked, half-hopeful as the anxiety slowly dissipated.

Max cleared his throat. "I had a long talk with Steven and the team at Journey yesterday," he explained. "A lot to catch you up on, actually—we caught the guy who leaked our stills. But the more important thing is, I'm going to be stepping down at Journey. I'll still own shares in the company and act as a consultant, but I want to be home. With Rosie. And you."

I felt my heart lurch forward.

"Oh," I breathed, staring at him in anticipation. "You—you're sure?"

His lips quirked up in that ridiculous half-smile I loved so much. My stomach fluttered with nerves and excitement, hoping this meant...

"I'm sure. This whole thing, you coming here, the mess at Journey, thinking I lost you again—it made me realize. I want you, Lacey. I want you here with me. I want you in Cold Springs and I want to take you out to get ice cream with me and Rosie. I want to sample all the food trucks in town with you. I want to sit on the couch with you and laugh and go for walks and hear all about your new job. And, I'm done with the press constantly badgering me about my love life."

He rushed on as a blush colored my cheeks, part excitement and part thrilled embarrassment.

"I know you're nervous about staying here, with me, and I understand that. But the offer is open. And if you get an apartment instead, that's great. I'm just happy you're staying. Because I've loved you since sophomore year of high school, Lacey Weaver, and I'll love you for the rest of my life."

There was a heavy, weighted moment of silence as we stood looking into each other's eyes. My brain was trying to catch up with it all, to make sense of it.

Max loved me.

All these years wasting time when I could have been... when I could have had...

Without a word, I launched myself into his arms and pressed my mouth to his. He let out an "umph" and caught me, arms tight around my waist. I grinned into the kiss and hoped for many, many nights together like the night we'd spent in his bed. Exhausted and satisfied, exhilarated and full of possibility.

"I love you too," I murmured, pulling back just enough to get the words out and see his lips lift in a smile.

Then I kissed him again. And again, and again, and again. I didn't ever want to stop kissing Max Munroe. No matter what the world threw our way.

Chapter 22

Epilogue

Six months later

Rosie was chattering excitedly in the back seat. He understood his daughter's excitement. It wasn't every day you moved into a new home.

Up ahead of them, the moving van pulled into the driveway and parked next to the garage. Two burly men got out, getting right to work with pulling open the back door. Move-in day was finally here.

From the passenger seat, Lacey turned and gave him a huge grin.

"Ready?" she asked, a hand on the door handle.

He nodded and opened his own door, watching Rosie dart off up the walkway and to the front door. The house in Ossett was small, but luxurious; understated. Mostly stone on the outside with big windows. Through the acre-and-a-half of trees, Max could just barely catch a glimpse of the lake.

At his side, Lacey took a deep breath.

"I can smell snow," she commented, giving him a warning look. "They checked the heat when they did the inspection, right?"

He laughed and nodded. "They did; checked everything. We should just have to unpack and… we're home."

Home.

He'd said the word a hundred, a thousand times in reference to the penthouse in Cold Springs. But this place actually felt like home. Maybe because it was a new beginning, or maybe because Lacey was here with him.

Their little trio felt like a family come full circle. Lacey and Skylar were even on decent speaking terms, coordinating time with Rosie.

"I'm going to see if they'll let me take some of the kitchen boxes, at least," Lacey said, pushing her glasses up her nose and grabbing her purse. She headed for the moving crew, giving them all a friendly smile, totally unaware of how absolutely gorgeous she was.

"Dad," Rosie said breathlessly, running up to him. "Keys!" She held out her hand and bounced on the balls of her feet. He stifled a chuckle, handing over the set of keys the realtor had given them this morning in Cold Springs.

It was only a forty-five minute drive away, but this felt like an entirely separate world from the city. Rosie would have to start at a new school, but his little girl was more excited than nervous. Lacey didn't have too bad of a drive into the city for her job at the library, especially considering she was working off-hours only four days a week.

And Max, well, he could consult right from home. Mostly for Journey, but he'd negotiated *not* signing a non-compete clause. Which meant he was free to work with whoever he wanted in the gaming and design industry.

Rosie ran up the sidewalk, joining Lacey, who opened the door for the movers. They maneuvered a decent sized nightstand in and Rosie followed, practically skipping. Lacey picked up a box labeled "kitchen" and headed in to start unloading and organizing.

Rosie asked Lacey when they were going to pick up their kitten. Rosie had picked out the most adorable brown tabby from the shelter. He had the cutest pink nose and was super cuddly. She had named him Geoffrey and they were holding him until we were able to bring him home. Rosie was over the moon excited about finally having a kitten to love.

Max stood for a few moments in silence. Or, near-silence.

He could hear birds chirping. And somewhere far off, the chatter and laughter of kids. Hopefully neighborhood kids that Rosie could make friends with.

His phone buzzed in his pocket and he pulled it out, seeing Steven's name on the screen.

"Hey," he answered, "everything good there?"

"Of course it is," Steven scoffed. "You know I'd never let your baby burn to the ground under Victor's dubious lead. But yeah, everything's going great—the designers are bringing some new storyboards to the meeting next week and we'll decide what our next big project is. Then I can start in on the budget."

"That's great," Max replied, blissfully stress-free. "Not to be rude, but what's up, then? We just got to Ossett and I want to try to get the bedrooms set up before nighttime."

Steven chuckled. "I was checking in to see if you reached out to that photographer Kate gave you the number for, for the proposal. You're on a tight deadline with this whole 'Christmas with the family' master plan, you know."

Max grinned, reminded once again of his elaborate plan for proposing to Lacey at her mom's place. He was planning on taking everyone out to the tree lighting in the small town and having a photographer nearby to capture the moment.

"Not yet, but I'll give her a call sometime tomorrow when Lacey is out of earshot."

"Good plan," he agreed. "Really good plan. And I think there's no chance that the press will figure out what you're doing and show up."

It was incredibly satisfying that, for once, his private life was truly private. There'd been a flurry of press interest when he'd publicly resigned as the CEO of Journey Studios, but it died down quickly. No one cared who he was dating.

Now that Max worked right from home, he spent the days with Rosie himself. Half-jokingly, he made comments about how he should have paid Lacey more. Raising a child could be exhausting. But yet, he couldn't be happier...

She always laughed it off and kissed him, responding that she got the best payoff ever. Finally getting together with him.

They were both achingly aware of just how bad they had it for one another, and Max wouldn't have it any other way.

Which, of course, was why he was going to propose.

"I'll call you back," he said, smiling as Lacey huffed out the front door to grab another box. "I've gotta help get everything settled. Talk soon?"

"Do what you've got to do," Steven said solemnly. "But I just want to say one more time for the record—I told you so."

And for once, Max didn't roll his eyes at his old friend's insistence that he and Lacey Weaver were head over heels for each other.

It was the absolute truth.

About Author

Alix loves everything about billionaires: confidence, luxury items, international travel and the immense power. Her characters usually come to her during a soak in a hot lavender-scented bath.

Her favorite things include expensive tequila, super dark chocolate, a walk in the woods and romance books you can't put down.

If you'd like to read a FREE book from Alix go to https://BookHip.com/NFXNJSC

Printed in Dunstable, United Kingdom

65405213R00099